THE BEYOND SERIES

Beyond
FOREVER

d. d. marx

Beyond Forever

Copyright © 2018 D. D. Marx

Contributors: Cover Illustration: Michael Fitzpatrick; Graphic Design by Morpheus Blak for Critical Mass Communications; Content Editor: Caroline Tolley; Copy Editor: Tim Jacobs Writing Consultants

ISBN: 978-0-9972481-2-8 paperback
ISBN: 978-0-9972481-5-9 ebook

Printed in the United States of America

To order, go to:
www.ddmarx.com

DEDICATION

Thank you, Danny!

BEYOND FOREVER

CHAPTER ONE
(OLIVIA)

"We are not going to cave when the doctor asks us if we want to know the sex of the baby, right? Do *not* let me cave. I want it to be a surprise," I say to Finn with nervous energy. I *hate* these appointments. They are so awkward and uncomfortable. If someone told me that I'd have a stranger shoving their full fist up past my ovaries and trying to tickle my tonsils every four weeks for almost a year, I might've been a little more diligent about swallowing my birth control pill on time. Don't get me wrong; I *want* this baby more than anything, but I just know it needs to come out *down there*.

"Aye, I'll throw myself in front of the sonogram machine if I see anything suspicious," my husband reassures.

"Everyone keeps telling me the way I'm carrying that it's a boy, but I think it's a girl." I'm not sure I would know what to do with a boy, having only grown up with my sister, Jane.

"The only kind of baby I want is a *healthy* one. I have no experience with either, so we'll figure it out together. Yer gonna be a great mum, Liv."

"Aw, thanks, love. I hope so. I can't believe we're sitting in the exam room at our six-month appointment. Nothing about *us* has gone according to plan."

"There's a *plan*?" Finn laughs.

"Good point. Nothing *but* surprises at every turn," I reply as the doctor enters.

"Good morning, Olivia."

"Good morning, Doctor Flanagan."

"How are you feeling? You look well," she says, glancing down at my chart.

"Thanks. I feel great."

"We got your blood work back. Everything looks normal. No diabetes. Blood pressure is right on target and your weight is in the range I would expect, so you're right on track."

"Wonderful."

"Let's get an ultrasound and some measurements to see how the baby's doing," she says, spreading warm jelly on my belly.

"We don't want to know the sex of the baby, so if you can avoid any show and tell, that would be appreciated."

"I'll do my best," she states, trying to get the equipment in place. "Baby's heartbeat is strong. Growth measurements look good. Here's a close-up of the baby's face. Smiling."

"Oh my gosh, Finn, *look* . . . and the baby has your nose. So sweet," I gush as we both tear up.

"Aye, brilliant," he whispers unable to contain his emotion.

I love watching Finn take in my pregnancy. He's so adorable. He waits on me hand and foot, always making sure I'm comfortable, have enough food, and getting enough sleep. He won't let me lift a finger. He's going to be the best dad. Deep down, he's a nervous wreck and rightfully so. He was on his way to becoming a dad and not only lost the baby but lost his wife, too. She was at the end of her first trimester when they thought she was having a miscarriage. The doctors went in and found her uterus full of cancer and had to perform an immediate hysterectomy. His hopes of becoming a father were shattered. He lost his wife, Christine, just a couple short years later after a valiant cancer battle.

Even through the pain, Finn and I know we are blessed beyond measure. We met when I was still reeling from the loss of my best friend from high school, Dan, in a car accident. Through a crazy twist of fate, our paths crossed. It was the right place and time when we were both longing for love the most. The best way to describe it is we were predestined. Early on, we discovered that Dan and Christine had been the best of friends in college. We know they are responsible for weaving the fabric of our lives together from the beyond. I want Finn to have faith that, this time around, everything will be fine. Dan and Christine are watching over us. They wouldn't *dare* let anything happen to this baby.

I'm flying from my new home in Palm Springs to my childhood stomping grounds, Chicago, this weekend. This is my last trip before the baby comes. My mom and my older sister, Jane, are throwing me a shower. Jane said my niece and nephew, Livey and Owen, are beside themselves about this baby coming. They are four-year-old twins and, by far, two of the biggest joys of my life. It's hard to imagine loving any child more, but that is the single most magical thing about the heart. Even with all the deep scars and gaping holes suffered throughout life, there's always more room for enormous love. *The ultimate cure-all.*

JANE: *Text me your flight information. The twins want to come with me to pick you up.*

OLIVIA: Oh good. I can't wait to see them. Flight 924 into Midway arriving at 10:15 a.m.

JANE: *We can't wait to see you. Safe flight. Love you!!*

OLIVIA: See you tomorrow. Love you, too!

As I exit baggage claim, I hear the kids yelling from the car at curbside pickup, "Auntie Liv, Auntie Liv." There is no sweeter sound. Jane helps me put my bag in the trunk then I climb in the back of the minivan to give the kids hugs, kisses, and snuggles.

"Is that the baby?" Livey asks, reaching out to touch my belly.

"Yes. Do you think it's a boy or girl?"

"A *girl*. When will she be out, so we can play with her?"

"I want a *booooy*," Owen shouts.

"Guess what? One of you is right. It's either a boy or girl. We don't know yet, but it won't be too much longer before you'll meet. This weekend we're going to have a party for the baby, so it knows what fun cousins you will be. How does that sound?"

"*Yeah*. Can we help open the presents?" Livey asks.

"Of course," I respond.

"Will there be a bouncy house at the party?" Owen chimes in.

"No, not at this party, buddy," I say with a giggle while I move up into the front seat.

"I have strict orders to deliver you straight to Mom and Dad's. They're dying to see you," Jane says as the kids start gabbing and singing. "They *live* for these kids and it won't be any different with this third grandbaby."

"I FaceTime them all the time so they can see the progress of the pregnancy, but it's not the same. They'd rather have me closer."

"You look terrific by the way. How are you feeling?"

"I must admit I've heard nightmare stories of the toll pregnancy can take on your body, but I feel incredible. Other than some brief morning sickness, I've been fortunate. My energy level is strong and our sex life is *on* fire," I whisper.

"I was the same way when I was pregnant with the twins." She glances in the rearview mirror to check on them.

"I was worried my sex drive would fall off a cliff when I found out I was pregnant a hot minute after the honeymoon, but it's added even *more* spice in the bedroom."

"Enjoy it now because once the baby gets here . . . good luck," Jane says with snark.

"Don't tell me that. *Seriously?*"

"Maybe it will be different for you guys, but all your focus shifts to the baby. You have someone else demanding your full attention, to take care of and worry about. At the end of the day, you're both so exhausted; all you'll want to do is sleep." She laughs. "*Trust* me."

"I *refuse* to be that couple. I am making a vow right now to plan date nights every other week to make sure we stay connected. I give you permission to perform frequent audits to ensure I stay true to my word." I grab my phone from my purse to text Finn to let him know I've arrived in Chicago safely.

"God bless you if you can." As we approach the red light across the street from our high school, "Small Town" starts to play on the radio.

"Unbelievable." Jane looks at me in complete disbelief.

"I know," I remark. "It's Dan's way of telling me he knows I'm home." "Small Town" is the song that reminds me most of Dan. The lyrics sum up his short but impactful life. Mellencamp was his favorite artist and the last concert we attended together. When he passed away, I was desperate to find a way to communicate with him. I asked him to send me "Small Town" anytime I need to feel him nearby, to let me know he's here with me. As I stare out the window at our high school, remembering our best memories, Dan lets me know he is with me. These are the moments that warm my heart and get me through the pain and agony. Grief is always lurking in the background and surfaces when you least expect it.

The memories come flooding back. The good old days of innocence and laughter when all we did was go to parties and concerts. Driving down the old, back-country roads with our windows down, blaring John Mellencamp without a care in the world. We had no idea we were on a timer. A timer that would expire without warning and take Dan away from me forever. All the emotion of that day settles in. We were on the phone together when a car crossed the middle lane and struck his car. The last time I ever heard his voice. The sharp, stinging pain of grief sears through me when Livey yells from the back seat.

"Turn it up," she demands and starts bopping in her car seat.

We arrive at my parents' house and exchange hugs and kisses. My mom made our favorite childhood comfort meal, tuna casserole. She made it every Friday night during Lent. It's a creamy mix of soupy, noodle deliciousness. *The perfect pregnancy food.*

"Now that we're all here, I have some news to share," Jane states.

"*Oh my God*, are you pregnant, too?" I quip. *Wouldn't it be hilarious if she stole my thunder?*

"*Nooo.* We just found out that . . . we're getting transferred to Austin, Texas."

"*What?* When?" I ask as I see my mom welling up with tears at the thought of her grandchildren moving away.

"Peter was promoted to SVP and they want him to move down to the corporate office," Jane explains.

"That's terrific news. This is a great opportunity for him," my dad interjects as my mom shoots him a glare.

"What about these babies? I can't be that far away from them," Mom whimpers.

"It's an amazing city, Mom. Much more affordable than Illinois. You guys can move, too. It's not Florida but a great place to retire. They have over three hundred days of sun. Dad can golf and fish, and I could certainly use the help with the kids. Peter will be working long hours and traveling with his team," Jane says, trying to soften the blow.

"Yeah, Mom. You guys could use a change. Get away from these winters. Remember how you fell in love with Austin when you were there for our wedding?

Why don't you and Dad take a trip and look at some areas? I'm sure Peter's company has a real estate firm they can recommend."

"Yes. We're going out to look for houses in a couple weeks. We can find someone to work with you," Jane offers. I can see by the look on my mom's face; she's already determined she will be going wherever the grandbabies are going, but my dad doesn't seem as sold on the idea.

"We'll have to think about it. This weekend is about celebrating this next grandbaby," Mom says. She is nervous. Her world is about to come crashing down. She can't imagine being without these grandchildren for a day. She changes the subject before she breaks down and my dad has the chance to shoot down the idea altogether. She changes the conversation by leaning down to rub my belly.

#

I get settled in my childhood room as the memories fill me up and cover me like a warm blanket. I call Finn.

"Hi, love," I say when he answers.

"Liv. I miss ye so much already. How ye feeling? How was the trip?"

"I hate being away from you. I wish you were here, but I know once the baby comes you'll need to take time away from the restaurant. I'll be home in a couple days. Trip was good. I feel fine. I had lunch with my parents, Jane, and the twins. Jane and Peter are being transferred to Austin."

"Really? How did yer folks handle the news?"

"Not great but we suggested they consider making a move, too. There's nothing keeping them here now, and the winters are so brutal. They need to downsize and live in a warmer climate. Plus, if we pursue opening another restaurant in Austin, we would be there quite a bit, too. How are things there?"

"Christine's is packed with reservations, which is good. Glad to be busy since ye aren't here. I'll take the night off on Tuesday so we can spend some time together when yer back."

"Sounds perfect. I love you."

"Love ye, too."

Christine's is the restaurant Finn opened in Palm Springs in honor of his late wife. After she passed, he was selected to compete on a reality cooking show called *Delectable*. He won a two hundred fifty-thousand-dollar prize and the head chef position at Mint in Las Vegas for a year. He rode out his contract with his sous chef Jimmy Bolt, whom we lovingly call Tex-Mex. They met on the show. When the year was up, they packed up together and moved to Palm Springs to start anew. They've been partners ever since.

#

I wake up to the sun shining on my face in the same room I spent all my awkward adolescent years. A few years ago, when I moved into my condo downtown, I encouraged my parents to redecorate my room, give it a fresh coat of paint and some new furniture. My mom kept making excuses about why they never did it. I think, deep down, she kept it the way it is so I would always have memories to come back to. To remember a time when I still had Dan. Right now, I'm grateful to see photos of his face surrounding me.

The baby shower starts at four, so I head over to the cemetery to pay Dan a visit in person. That constant feeling of needing to visit him has slowly faded. There was a time I went every week but since I've moved away, it's rare. I feel him around me enough to know he is always with me no matter where I am, but this trip is special. I want him to see the baby up close.

Hi, Danny. How are you? I run my fingers over the top of his smooth, gray marble headstone and give it a kiss. *It's been a while.* Tears fall from my eyes.

I miss you. Am I ever going to get over the disbelief of you being gone forever? What would we be doing if you were still here? Would you be married? Would your wife be pregnant, too? Would our kids grow up together? Would we have drifted apart? Maybe we'd be so busy and wrapped up in our own lives that we'd only see each other at holidays and talk on our birthdays. I can't imagine that would be the case, but time is a luxury we take for granted. I have a constant reminder of how precious it is and how much every second should be treasured. Okay, enough sappy talk. Here is the baby. I rub my belly.

I think it's a girl, but everyone else is convinced it's a boy. I don't care. I want a happy, healthy baby. It's been such a wonderful experience feeling this human being moving and growing inside of me. Sometimes I pretend you're giving me a swift kick when I need it. I laugh.

So, the real reason I'm here is because Finn and I have a very important question we want to ask of you and Christine, which is why I waited to come in person. We want you to be the baby's godparents. We know you're always watching over us, but we want you to love and protect this little one with everything you have. You are now guardian angels, so it's the only thing that feels right — for both of us.

Just as I finish, the sun darts out from behind a cloud like a glistening smile and a warm hug. *Perfect, I'll take that as an emphatic YES. We love you.*

I get in the car, turn on the ignition, and hear "Oh, oh, oh / Sweet child o' mine / Oh, oh, oh, oh / Sweet love of mine" playing by Guns N' Roses.

You never cease to amaze me, Danny. I burst into tears.

CHAPTER TWO
(FINN)

Liv arrives back from Chicago this afternoon. I take Frank for a run, shower, and am rushing to get into the restaurant to prep for the day so I can leave early to pick her up. I'm making her a nice dinner so we can spend some quality time together. We are officially on a timer. We only have so much *us* time left before we become three.

While en route, I get a call from Tex.

"Scottie, ya on your way in?" he asks.

"Aye. What's up, lad?"

"Was hoping to catch ya in time. Can ya swing by the farmers' market and pick up some more scallions? Seems our delivery is a bit light this week."

"Aye. No problem. We need anything else?" I ask.

"Nope, that should do it. See you soon."

I make the quick pit stop, arrive at the restaurant, and as I walk in the back door, all I hear is "SURPRISE" as the staff jumps out from their hiding spots in the kitchen.

"What's this?" I ask, scanning the room. I see Tex; Garrett and his partner, Tristan; Mac, my best lad from growing up; his wife, Jules; and then lock eyes with Liv. She flew back early to surprise me.

"Hi, love," she says.

"Are ye my surprise?" I say, pulling her in for a hug and kiss.

"Sort of. Everyone wanted to throw you a 'man shower.' It's a baby shower focused on the dad. The team felt bad we didn't have a local baby shower and wanted to do something for us. When they reached out to me, I told them I wanted it to be focused on you," Liv says.

"*Brilliant.* Thank ye. I don't know the first thing about these so I guess let's start showering," I announce.

The restaurant is decked out with baby decorations. Bunches and bunches of pink and blue balloons at every turn. A wall strung with bibs, onesies, socks, wash cloths, and diapers. You name it, they thought of it. No doubt Garrett had a hand in this. He has lanterns hung from the ceiling. Floral centerpieces, in the shape of a rattle, adorn each table and the place settings are made into little baby carriages. *I can't believe they pulled it off.* This might be the last time we see everyone in one place before the baby arrives.

"I reckon we got ya," Tex teases as he and his girlfriend, Christie, greet me near the bar while Liv's mingling.

"Scallions, eh?"

"I needed to stall ya. Liv was still on her way, so I needed to buy another twenty minutes. I reckon it worked out perfect."

"I didn't suspect a thing. I'm really touched. Thank you."

"You're welcome, and, speaking of surprises, I actually have another one for ya."

"Oh, what's that?"

"Christie and I got engaged last night."

"That's *bloody fantastic*. Congratulations, lad. Couldn't happen to a greater couple." I embrace them both. "When's the big day?"

"We don't want a long engagement. We're thinking about eloping and having our reception here at Christine's. After all, this is where it all started," he says.

"That would be glorious. Whatever you want. I'm sure it wouldn't take much convincing to get Garrett involved. He loves getting his hands dirty and will transform this place," I add.

"We can talk more. . . but today is about you and this baby, so I reckon we have some celebratin' to do."

Tex met Christie at an ALS fundraiser we had here at the restaurant several months ago. She is local to the area and they hit it off immediately. I'm happy Tex found his match. He's put his blood, sweat, and tears into this restaurant the last couple years and hasn't taken much time for himself. I've been hoping he'd find someone and settle down. Palm Springs isn't much of a singles' town, especially for a guy that works sixteen-hour days. These are the moments when you believe fate exists. Christie walked into his life out of nowhere, just like Liv did into mine.

I give a toast to Tex and Christie's impending nuptials and we enjoy the afternoon. We nibble on tapas, a scrumptious cake, and open gifts. The staff was more than generous. They bought us all the large items remaining on the baby registry: the car seat, high chair, and stroller, but the most touching gift by far was a sweet, delicate mobile made of angels for the crib. The angels have satin wings and are holding gold horns, but they had it customized to play the music from the song "I'm Your Angel" by Celine Dion. To add to it, they had a wooden sign personalized for the baby's room. It's painted in a soft pink color and decorated with whimsical angel wings that read: *Guardian Angels Pure and Bright, Guard Me as I Sleep Tonight.* We are so incredibly touched that they would go to such lengths to express their love and joy for this baby. There is not a dry eye.

#

We arrive home mid evening. "Do ye still want me to make ye dinner, or would ye like to get straight to dessert?" I ask Liv, kissing her neck.

"Mm, that sounds heavenly. How about a bubble bath? We'll be using that tub for a different purpose in a few short months," she laughs.

"Please take a load off, Mrs. McDaniels, while I draw you a bath."

We are still in the honeymoon phase. The pregnancy has only enhanced Liv's sex drive, which is lucky for me since I can't get enough of her. She becomes sexier every single day. There isn't anything more beautiful than seeing the woman you love carrying your baby. It's the most glorious sight. I feel so blessed and grateful. I don't want to ever take what we have for granted. She's my everything. After a lingering sensual bath, we make love and drift off to sleep.

I wake up in the middle of the night, startled and sweating.

Liv sits up. "Honey, you must've had a nightmare. You okay?" She rubs my back as I catch my breath and grab for the glass of water on my night stand.

"I don't know," I reply as images of the terrorist attack come rushing back.

"*What?* What is it?"

"No, no, it's nothing; go back to sleep," I say then lay back down and roll over. I don't want to worry her, but I lay there wide awake until morning. It's almost as if I'm willing myself to stay awake so I don't have to see those horrid images again.

#

"Good morning love," I say, approaching the bed with a tray full of all of Liv's favorites: bacon, eggs, Texas toast with butter, and a tall glass of orange juice. The sun is piercing through the window at just the right angle to highlight her face. She's still snuggled in the down duvet with her head buried in her pillow. I love seeing her early in the morning without her makeup and her hair tousled. She looks adorable.

"What do I owe the pleasure?" She sits up in bed, inhaling the fresh, crispy bacon. "You should use bacon as an aphrodisiac more often."

"Mental note taken but right now I want ye to rest. Ye've been traveling and ye should take it easy today."

"Can you call in sick and join me?" she begs, playfully pulling me back into bed, careful not to spill her tray.

"We've never had a lazy day, have we?" I reply, thinking about the pace of our relationship and how quickly everything moved. We were apart for most of the time we were dating. When we were together, we were busy, running around. Neither of us relax. We're both doers, go-getters. Relaxation is a foreign concept.

"Come to think of it, no. It's been a bit of a whirlwind since the day we met, hasn't it?" She answers my internal questions, coming to the same realization.

"Then your wish is my command, my love. Tex can handle things at the restaurant. Today is officially Liv Day. Whatever ye want to do," I offer.

"Okay, then let's cuddle up with Frank and watch old sappy romantic comedies all day."

"Sounds heavenly," I reply.

"But first, I want to ask you something. I've noticed you've been restless while sleeping for the last several weeks. I chalked it up to you having a lot on your mind with the baby coming but after last night, I'm sensing it might be deeper than that. What's really going on?" Liv pats the bed, gesturing for me to crawl back into bed to lay next to her.

"I don't want to worry you."

"That sounds serious," she says, reaching for me to pull me closer.

"Nah, I haven't mentioned it only because I didn't want to give it legs. So please know this was never something I was deliberately keeping from ye, okay? We don't have any secrets; I promise ye."

"Okaaay."

"Remember when I told you what the doctor said? Due to my head injury during the terrorist attack, I could start experiencing flashbacks? Things that my mind suppressed in the moment due to the impact and the shock to my body?"

"Yes."

"Ever since we got back to California, post recovery, I've been having a recurring dream. I'm not sure if this is considered a flashback since it's occurring in my subconscious, but it's the same each time. I'm back in the Charles de Gaulle Airport, walking toward baggage claim. I'm right behind a young dad holding his little daughter's hand. Then the blast hits and they get separated. I start frantically searching for each of them so I can help reunite them. I'm walking over a sea of bodies when I see the little girl. When I reach for her hand, Christine appears as if she's there to take her to heaven."

"Oh, honey. . ." she says, rubbing my chest to comfort me. "Wow."

"I always wake up the moment I see Christine. That's why I'm so startled. It's shocking. I feel like it is *her*."

"There's research that says when you see a loved one in your dreams, it's a visitation. You've been through several traumatic events. I mean, you lost the baby, then Christine, and, of all things, a terrorist attack. I can't *believe* what you've been through."

"I just feel like . . . like . . ." I hesitate.

"Like what?"

"Like she's coming to warn me about something that will happen to ye or the baby."

"Finn, don't you *dare* say that. No. *Noooo*. There is no way. Maybe you're looking at this the wrong way. What if she's coming to let you know that she's okay and on the other side with your baby, and they are the ones who protected you during the attack?"

"That's certainly a more positive way of looking at it. I guess I tend to go to the dark side."

"I'm the same way. I always think the worst. It's a defense mechanism. We've both been through a lot. We're trying to protect ourselves." She pauses. "But I have an idea that might make you feel better."

"Making love to you?" I joke.

"Of course, we can work that in, but I'm thinking more along the lines of you scheduling an appointment with that psychic I went to the night of our first date. Her store is across from Tracy's salon, Mayne. I can make you an appointment. It might bring you comfort to see if Christine comes through."

"Let's talk about that later. Right now, I have more urgent plans," I say, reaching over and grazing my fingertips over her nipples.

"You're impossible, Finn McDaniels."

I'm on my way to the medium reading that Liv made me. I mean, I believe, of course, but I have doubts. *Are the signs we get from our loved ones coincidences, or things we create to make us feel better?* I want to believe Christine is here with me, but right now I'm most afraid of what I might hear — especially any bad news. What if she tells me I'm going to have a heart attack and die at a young age? I'd rather live blissfully unaware of my impending doom. I start taking long, deep breaths relax then begin switching the car radio channels, frantically trying to distract my rambling thoughts. That's when I land on a station and "Small Town" is playing. *See, this is exactly what I'm talking about. Is this a coincidence? How often does "Small Town" get air play?* There's a good chance I could hear it on any average day, but now I'm hearing it on my way to talk to Dan and Christine. These are the events that give you hope that our loved ones are still around and are always connected to us. As I pull into the parking lot, I find a spot and turn the car off.

Christine, please help me get through this. Give me something concrete so I know you're here with me. Something undeniable and impossible for me to refute. What I want most is to know that everything is going to be okay with Liv and the baby. I cannot bear to go through any more trauma. I don't know why I keep having these nightmares. What are you trying to tell me? Please help me understand what it is I'm sensing. I will always love you. Tell Dan I say hi and thanks for the Mellencamp surprise. Here goes nothing!

When I open the door, I'm overwhelmed by the scent of burning candles. *Lavender.* A calm comes over me. The smoke in the air is soothing, almost angelic. A woman approaches me and introduces herself.

"Hi, I'm Kelly, you must be Finn," she says, extending her hand.

"Aye. Nice to meet ye, Kelly." I shake her hand.

"Don't be nervous. I promise this won't hurt," she says, laughing.

"Aye, thank ye. I've never done anything like this before, so I must admit I'm quite nervous."

"Most people who come to see me leave here feeling much better than when they arrived. Hopefully that gives you some comfort." She gestures for me to follow her back to the room where she'll do the reading. As we walk in, I can see how Liv connected here. The room is quaint but homey and inviting.

"Please have a seat," she says. "I'm not sure you know anything about my process, but I'm going to ask you to sit here quietly for a couple of minutes to clear your mind. I want you to come up with three wishes. Ask for one specific thing you would like for your loved one to present to you during the reading to validate it is them. I find that process clears the mind and leaves you more open to receiving whatever messages may be waiting for you."

"Okay," I say as I close my eyes.

My three wishes are the following:

1. *To keep Liv and our unborn baby healthy, safe, and fulfilled forever. I want Liv to realize her dreams and continue to inspire me by reaching for the stars.*

2. *For me to be the man of Liv's dreams, to continue to earn her love, respect and trust, to never, ever take her or our love for granted, and to be the best da and provider to my children. Someone they are proud to call their husband and da.*

3. *My last wish is for Liv and me to live free from fear. To live a life knowing that God through our own guardian angels, Dan and Christine, is protecting us and the ones we love, and will continue to give us strength and prosperity on our journey.*

"Okay, I'm ready," I say to Kelly.

"Let's get started." She closes her eyes and places her hands over mine while whispering a prayer. "Spirit, please protect Finn and guide him with your love and light, in all things good, always and forever. Amen."

"Amen." Kelly has a notebook next to her where she takes down notes and sketches symbols as she is receiving them. She is an unassuming woman, a little older, attractive, and has a pleasant and inviting demeanor. She is confident with what she is saying but not forceful. It's as if she is seeing it at the same time she's saying it. I do sense she is connecting, which is calming my nerves.

"Wow, right away I have someone here who is eager to get through. A young female in her early twenties. Do you know who this would be?"

"Aye," I say, catching my breath.

"She is holding her hands over her chest, which is my symbol indicating she passed with something related to that area? Is that correct?"

"Aye. She passed away from breast cancer."

"She wants to say thank you for loving her and taking care of her. She knows how hard it was for you to let her go but she is at peace. There was nothing that could have been done. Any additional treatment would have prolonged the inevitable. You gave her permission to be free from pain."

"*Brilliant*," I say, welling up with tears.

"She's holding a little boy's hand and wants you to know they are together on the other side."

I am almost paralyzed in disbelief. *Glorious, it was a baby boy.*

"Incredible. We lost a baby, but we never knew if it was a boy or girl."

"She wants me to tell you how proud she is of you and all of your accomplishments. She's showing me a leaf . . . like an herb of some sort. Hmmm, this is weird. I've never seen this one before. It looks like something you would *cook* with? Like a green, leafy herb. Does that make sense?"

"Is it by chance, mint?"

"Yes! That's exactly what it is."

"After she passed, I was on a cooking reality show and won a head chef position at a restaurant in Vegas called Mint. That's amazing . . . *wow.*"

"I'm hearing the name Frank. Do you know who that would be?"

"Aye. That was her nickname in college and I have a golden retriever named Frank, after her." I smile. This is truly mind blowing. I had no idea she would be or could be so specific. There's no way Kelly could know any of this. She's hitting everything right on the head.

Before she ends our session, she asks, "Is there anything else you want to know or want to ask?"

"Aye. Two things. The first—is she with anyone besides the little boy in heaven?"

"Let me check. Okay, yes, I'm hearing the name Danny. Do you know who that would be?"

"Aye, brilliant. That's exactly what I wanted to hear. My last question is related to my recent recurring dreams. Is everything going to be all right with Liv and the baby?"

"All she is saying is . . . trust me . . . over and over."

"Thank ye so much. Ye've answered my questions."

"Is this what you expected?" she asks as she escorts me back up to the front lobby.

"I'm still trying to process everything but yes, more than I imagined. Very specific. Astonishing. Thank ye again," I reply.

"Connecting people with their loved ones brings me tremendous joy. I'm glad you got what you needed. I hope it brings you peace, knowing that they are always with us. Take comfort in the signs. Believe they are real and have faith in their messages."

Amazing. Thank you, Christine. You still take my breath away. I love you forever.

Chapter Three
(OLIVIA)

"*Finnnnnn,*" I yell, catching my breath. *This is happening.*

"Aye. What is it love?" He rushes into the bedroom to see what's wrong.

"My water just broke," I blurt out in disbelief. My mind is flooded with everything that's not done. I mean, we're ready but we're not *ready, ready.* I'm not due for two more weeks and I assumed I'd be late, so we haven't done the test drive to the hospital or packed my bag. Finn hasn't set up the bassinet. We still need to wash the clothes from the baby shower. I haven't decided which outfit I want the baby to leave the hospital in. Most importantly, my vagina is *definitely not ready.*

"Stay calm. Deep breaths. We can do this. What do you need?"

"*More time is what I need. . .*" I screech.

"Have the contractions started?" Finn asks nervously.

"No, not yet, but the doctor said to go straight to the hospital if this happened."

"Aye, right. Let's get ye in the car and I'll pack your bag."

"I have enough time to pack a bag. I don't need thong underwear and a negligee, which is what you would pack." I chuckle. "Sorry to snap, honey. Reality is setting in and fear is taking over."

"Liv, darling, it's all going to be okay. I'm right here. I've got ye." He leans over to give me a sweet kiss.

"I love you so much."

"I love ye, too. We're leaving here as two and comin' home as three."

"Awww, now you're gonna make me cry," I say, tearing up. My emotions are all over the place, hormones raging. One minute I'm elated, then sad, followed by terrified and everything in between. *Is this normal?* I can't believe the moment is *here. Of course, I can't wait to meet the baby, but what if I'm a terrible mom? What if I'm not equipped to raise a child? What if the baby hates me?* I haven't even decided if I'm breastfeeding yet. I feel like there are still so many big decisions and choices to make. I'm a planner by nature. I'm not comfortable in the unknown, and as soon as I enter that hospital, there is nothing but unknown ahead of me. Lesson number one catapulting me into parenthood. *Danny, I need to feel you, now. HELP!*

"Aye. I'll stop yapping. I'll be in the car. T minus five minutes. Get what you need."

#

Finn is driving the speed limit and following all the rules of the road given the precious cargo on board. He's acting completely adorable, which is not out of the norm but sometimes I forget to appreciate this part of him. He's quite the protector. His natural instincts are kicking in. I know deep down he is more frightened than me. He's trying to put on a strong demeanor to keep me calm.

We arrive at the hospital and are escorted to our room by wheelchair. I have a private room and get settled in bed as the nurses hooked me up to monitor all my vitals. It's too early for an epidural since contractions haven't started and I'm only two centimeters dilated. Finn sends out a group text to let everyone know that we are at the hospital and the baby is on its way. He steps out to call his parents. Meanwhile, my mind is still in a frenzy. I can't stop thinking about the last thing I ate and how much I'll poop all over the doctor during labor. Women do this all the time. *How do they not obsess about all this stuff? Why didn't anyone buy me the book called All the shit no one tells you about pregnancy? — pun intended.*

Right before I'm about to start hyperventilating, Garrett bursts into the room. Garrett Stanford is my cousin and dearest friend. His mere presence brings me comfort.

"Sweetie. Oh my God, it's happening. How are you?" he says, leaning over to give me a hug.

"Ohhhhh, thank God you're here. I'm freaking out but trying to keep it together for Finn so I don't scare him," I admit.

"I passed him in the hallway."

"He's calling his parents. On that topic, I told everyone to reach out to you for updates so we don't overwhelm Finn. Is that okay?"

"Of course, you know me, I *love* delivering news. *Gay Handbook* Rule #1 — owner of drama, no matter what kind! So, are the contractions bad?"

"Haven't started. My water broke," I say as he gasps.

"*Ewww.* Did it explode on anything important?" He cringes.

"Leave it to you to make this whole giving-birth thing gross. *No.* None of your precious decor is tainted with placenta. I was in the bedroom. It started as a small leak, so I was able to make it into the bathroom in time."

"Oh, thank God. Did you have time for a pedi and wax to pretty everything up for the doctor?"

"Ummm, no. I hadn't even *thought* about that but thanks for piling it on. I'm already freaking out that this baby has to exit through my vajayjay," I say, disgusted.

"Honey, I know nothing on the subject, so spare me the details. Can't you pay a little extra for a C-section?" Garrett asks.

"Unfortunately, it doesn't work that way, but thanks for the suggestion," I say as Finn walks back in.

"Laddie, so good to see ye. Thanks for comin'," he says to Garrett.

"Wouldn't miss it. Huge day for the McDaniels."

"I saw the nurse come in. Any progress?" Finn asks.

"No, I'm not dilating fast enough, so they're about to start Oxytocin to induce labor. The anesthesiologist should be in shortly to start an epidural. Why don't you and Garrett go grab something to eat? I'm going to try to close my eyes for a bit to get some rest and kill some time. It might be the most uninterrupted sleep I get for the next eighteen years."

"Aye. We'll be downstairs in the café. Text me *the second* you feel anything."

"Promise. Love you."

"Love ye, too. Get some rest." He gives me a sweet kiss.

I send a group text off to the girls: Jane, Red, Liza, and Alexa. Red, Susan Graham, is my other best friend from high school. Dan's thing was to give everyone he knew a nickname. The nickname Red since she has auburn hair. My nickname was Hank. Short for Henry, Olivia Henry. Alexa is my college sorority sister from the University of Dayton, and Liza is her cousin, who I met on a plane when returning from the start of my whirlwind romance with Finn. They are the best girlfriends anyone could ask for. Liza and Alexa live in Cincinnati. Red lives with her husband in Chicago. We don't get to see each other as often as I would like but we're as thick as thieves. They've been on baby watch for the last month so I know they are anxious for an update.

OLIVIA: Hi Girlies. It's happening!!!!! I know Finn texted earlier but I am officially in labor. They started me on Oxytocin to speed things up and contractions have begun. I had an epidural so feeling no pain. Garrett is here, and he and Finn just ran to grab food. Going to try to get some shut eye while it's quiet. Will keep you posted. Love you!

Red: Keep us posted. We love you!

Jane: The kids are screaming! YAY!

Alexa: 1 . . . 2 . . . 3 . . . puuuuuush. Can't wait to see pics!

Liza: Good Luck! XO

#

Contractions start kicking in more frequently and I am now seven centimeters dilated. Although I'm not in pain, I can feel lots of pressure. The doctor is performing internal exams every hour as I get closer. Finn is taking his cues from me. He's heard about pregnant women freaking out on their husbands because they are at fault for the pain being inflicted. Men do have it *so easy*. I would never do that to him but it's fun watching him squirm. He's been keeping everyone up to date on my status. My parents have tickets to fly out just after my due date. No one expected me to go early. I hope they can move it up so my mom can come help me when I get out of the hospital.

"Finn, I'm starting to get this warm, itchy feeling over me," I say nervously as the baby heart monitor starts to increase in pace. My blood pressure and heart monitor machines start beeping. I see the frantic look on Finn's face then hear him yell "Doctor!" as everything goes black.

The next thing I know, I feel myself floating. I'm looking down at my body on the operating room table. Doctors are in a frenzy. I hear them say, "She's crashing" as they start CPR. I'm losing a lot of blood as I see them going in to take the baby. *What is happening? Am I dead?* And I look up and there he is. Dan is standing next to me.

"*DANNY!*" I sob, squeezing him as hard as I can.

"HANK, *hi*," he says, embracing me tight. "We don't have a lot of time."

"What do you mean? Where am I?" All I can see is a bright light but I can't see past Dan. We're in this alternate state. It's hard to describe. I can see and hear everything happening below me in the room but no one can see or hear me.

"You're at the gates of heaven but you're not supposed to be here yet."

"Why? What's happening?" I take in every detail of him. He looks exactly as I remember. His sandy blonde hair, piercing baby blue eyes, and that smile with dimples for days. *Perfection.* He looks electrifying. Himself but only a million times better.

"Your heart stopped. You've lost a lot of blood but the doctors will work hard to bring you back. You will be fine."

"But I don't know if I want to go back. I've missed you so much. I can't say goodbye again." I am paralyzed with emotion. I am so overwhelmed that he's right here with me.

"Your baby girl needs you."

"Baby girl? But we don't know what we're having." We look down and see the doctors deliver the baby while they continue working to revive me.

"It's a beautiful, healthy baby girl. She needs you and Finn needs you . . . now more than ever."

"Thank you so much for finding him for me, Danny. I love him *so* much. I can't leave him. He wouldn't be able to take the sadness. He'd never recover. He misses Christine so much, too. Is she with you?"

"Finn was always planned as a part of *your* future. Even before you were born. There is always a plan. And yes, Christine is with me but wasn't allowed to come. We are together on the other side."

"What's it like? Heaven?" I beg.

"It's indescribable. Magical. Brilliant. Vibrant. The most glorious place you've ever seen."

"I love and miss you so much . . . you know that, right?"

"Yes, and me too, Hank. But you need to know, I am *always* with you. In every moment. I will watch out for you and protect you from harm for all of eternity. It's my job on the other side. I'm a guardian angel to the ones I loved the most. The ones I left behind."

"Really? So, you can hear me when I talk to you and ask you for things?"

"Yes, but I'm only allowed to respond with signs and symbols. You're one of the lucky ones. You're in tune and learning how I communicate. You need to continue to trust and have faith. There are so many good things ahead for you and Finn. I promise. And I assure you, Christine and I will be the best godparents we can be to Danielle Christine."

"Oh, Danny, you can hear and see me." I hug him, never wanting to let go.

"I know everything, even before you do. I am guiding you Hank, but you must go. We must say goodbye for now. I will love you forever and always. We'll be together again someday, I promise."

"I love you too, *so, so, so very much.*"

"And Hank, God only has one rule, which allowed me to be here with you."

"What is it?"

"When you wake up, you won't remember our encounter. See you in your dreams." And with that he was gone.

#

There is pressure on my chest and through my subconscious I hear doctors talking. No matter how hard I try, I can't open my eyes. All I want to do is sleep forever.

Chapter Four
(FINN)

Dan and Christine, I'm imploring you . . . PLEASE help them. You can't take them from me. Neither of them. Why is this happening? Haven't we all been through enough? When will it be over? When can we start living? Believing? Trusting? I just want to breathe again — live, love, and laugh without the fear of something bad happening. I know there are so many good things out there. We just need to find them. I am putting every ounce of my faith in you in this exact moment. Christine, you told me to trust you so that's what I'm going to do. I promise if they pull through that we will name her in your honor. Whatever it takes. I will move past the old me and lead my life with passion and positivity. Liv is my soulmate. My best friend. My everything. I need her here with me . . . forever. Please, please help me. I need you to show me a sign that they will be okay.

Just as I finish my prayer, my phone buzzes in my pocket. I pull it out to find a text from Liv. All it says is *I love you*. It must be delayed because of the spotty Wi-Fi here in the hospital. She must have sent it when Garrett and I went to get food. Before I have a chance to collapse in relief, Garrett appears.

"I just left for a minute and got your text. Oh my God, what happened?" Garrett says, returning from taking a quick call when he sees the panic-stricken look on my face.

"It's Liv. One minute we were sitting in the room and waiting for her to finish dilating, then everything fell apart. She said she felt warm and tingly then her monitors started going haywire, so I called for the nurse. Before I knew it, they whisked her off to the OR for an emergency C-section. They said she and the baby were both in distress. They wouldn't let me go in with them." I am distraught as I pace in the hallway outside the waiting room.

"And you still don't have any update?" Garrett asks.

"Nah and I can barely breath." I'm numb.

"Let me get you some water. I'll find a nurse to see if we can get any information. You stay here." He darts off to find someone. Just as all my darkest fears come flooding back, I see Garrett approaching with Liv's doctor.

"Doctor, how are they?" I say, trembling.

"They are both . . . *fine*," the doctor says, grabbing my hands. "Olivia and the baby were in distress so we performed an emergency C-section. Olivia was losing blood very quickly so we had to give her a transfusion, but we did deliver the baby without incident. Not to alarm you but due to the shock to Olivia's system, she did briefly go into cardiac arrest. We administered CPR and she responded instantly. She hasn't suffered any long-term complications. It's what we call an acute incident. She will, however, need a lot of rest for the next few weeks to regain her strength."

"Brief cardiac arrest? Are you saying she *died*?" I say in disbelief.

"Yes, technically her heart stopped but it was *very* brief. I assure you: she will be totally fine."

I fall back into my chair.

"Aye. Thank ye, Doctor. Liv is my whole life. I cannot thank ye enough."

"The wonderful news is you have a beautiful, healthy baby *girl*. You can go see her in the nursery. Olivia will be in recovery for several more hours, being closely monitored, but she is out of the woods," the doctor reassures me. Garrett and I lock eyes as the doctor leaves.

"Finn, *oh my God*. Are you okay?" he asks, sitting down to comfort me.

"Stunned. If I weren't so speechless, I'd have asked the doctor more questions. Right now, I'm grateful it's over and I want to get my hands on my precious daughter. Care to join me?"

"No, you go. I'll wait here in case there's any more news on Liv," Garrett says.

"Have ye updated anyone?" I ask.

"No, I didn't want to frighten anyone, especially since we didn't know what was going on."

"Aye. I think we should wait until yer aunt and uncle get here before we tell them about the events that unfolded. I don't want them to worry. I'll send everyone a text letting them know that the baby is here, and that she and Liv are resting. I'll get photos and send along more details later."

"Do you guys have a name picked out?" he asks.

"We do but I'll let Liv have that moment. She'll be exhausted but sharing the news will lift her spirits."

"Let me know whatever you need," he replies.

I arrive at the nursery and spot the pink cap and incubator labeled *McDaniels*. The nurse approaches the window and I show her my wristband, authorizing my access. She invites me in, shows me to a big, comfortable chair in a quiet area, where I can have some privacy, and then hands me my brand-new baby girl. I'm in awe and overcome with emotion as tears stream down my cheek. I'm elated, joyful, fearful, relieved, anxious, and hesitant all rolled into one. I've never felt such abounding love. She's so tiny and fragile. I'm afraid if I squeeze too hard I'll break her.

"Hi sweet darling, it's me. Your da. Ye've given your mum and me quite the scare, little one. I hope this doesn't mean yer going to be trouble as a teenager. Either way, you will always be daddy's little girl. I love ye to infinity and beyond. Do us a favor and be patient with us because we've never done this before, okay? I know yer mum can't wait to hold and smother ye. She's resting now but we'll see her soon," I whisper, covering her with endless kisses.

Thank ye, Dan and Christine. She's sublime.

I sit with her for what feels like an eternity. I feed her her first bottle. Surreal is the only word to describe this moment, which is not at all how I pictured it. I thought we'd be in a private delivery room. I'd be kissing Liv after I shouted "It's a girl," cut the umbilical cord, and we'd have our first look at her together. Although she didn't arrive the way we expected, I'm holding my perfect little angel in my arms and vow to protect her for all my remaining days. I am now quite certain I understand the definition of unconditional love. Her eyes are closed. She is resting so peacefully, considering the chaos around her when she appeared. Her breathing is soft and content. She is pure, unmarred, and full of innocence. Everything about her is gentle and delicate. Her tiny fist wraps around my pinky and I am taken aback by her strength, which she clearly inherited from Liv. I can't wait for her to meet her amazing mum but for now I treasure every passing second.

#

Liv is finally transferred to a room but isn't alert yet. They have her on oxygen. She is still connected to monitors for her vitals. The spacious, private room is equipped with a bathroom, shower, and a couch that folds out into a bed. I'll be able to stay here with her until it's time to go home in a few days. I never thought to bring a bag with me. Nothing about *us* ever goes according to plan. I think our best quality as a couple. They brought in the baby to be with me. I will feed her by bottle until Liv determines if she has the strength to breastfeed. Once I settle in, I call both sets of parents to give them the update about the unexpected C-section, minus the cardiac arrest, the baby's measurements, and to let them know Liv is resting. I mention that we haven't announced the name because we were waiting to meet her first before deciding.

It's the middle of the night when Liv wakes up.

"Finn. . ." she whispers.

"Aye, darling," I respond, startled. I must have dozed off in the chair next to the bed. I lean over to kiss her. "How was yer sleep?"

"Where is the baby? I don't remember anything," she asks, looking around.

"Stay still." I pick the baby up from the incubator and place her in Liv's arms. "It's a *girl*."

"*Really?* Look at her. She is absolute perfection . . . *hi sweetie*." She weeps, uncovering the swaddled blanket to see all ten of her fingers and toes.

"Indeed."

"What happened?" she asks.

"You and the baby went into distress and in a flash, they were speeding you off to perform an emergency C-section. I couldn't go in with ye because . . . well, because . . . it was life threatening." She looks up at me with giant eyes.

"*Life threatening?*"

"Aye." I fill her in on the details as gently as I can.

"Oh Finn, my love, I am *soooo* sorry to put you through a scare like that. I can't imagine the agony you must have been going through," she says, pulling me in closer for a hug and kiss.

"I won't lie. It was the longest twenty minutes of my life but Garrett was here with me. I begged Dan and Christine to take care of ye both. Thank God they answered my prayers."

"What about this little angel? Did the trauma affect her?" she asks, cuddling the baby.

"No, she handled it like a champ — just like her mum. My two fighters."

"And you had all those premonitions. *Wow.* I can't believe I *died.* I wonder if I saw Dan? The last thing I remember is laying in my room and being dilated at seven centimeters."

"I haven't shared that detail. I didn't want to freak anyone out. Yer mum and da will be here the day we get released so we can tell them in person. The doctor said ye must stay an extra day and will need plenty of rest once ye get home. Yer body has been through a lot and ye lost a lot of blood."

We sit in silence. I can see her mind spinning as she processes the magnitude of what happened.

"What are we going to name her?" she asks, looking back at the baby. Her maternal instinct is already kicking in. She must be so weak, sore, and exhausted but you would never know it.

"During the chaos, I sorta promised Dan and Christine that if ye pulled through we would name her Danielle Christine and call her Dani. Dani McDaniels. It has a bit of a ring to it, doesn't it?"

"The name your mom tried to avoid by naming you Finn? I wouldn't want it any other way. It suits her perfectly and is the only appropriate tribute to her very special guardian angels."

#

The doctor comes in to check on Liv.

"Good morning," she says, picking up Liv's chart. "How are you feeling? You look a little pale, which is expected."

"I feel okay, just tired and a little bit unsteady," Liv responds.

"I presume your husband filled you in on the events of yesterday?"

"Yes, I was shocked. I didn't realize how quickly everything changed."

"Fortunately, we have a highly skilled medical team so you weren't in danger for long. On a positive note, I didn't even tell Finn this but the baby came out smiling, almost smirking, as if she'd just been told a secret. Many of the medical staff commented on how unusual it was. Sadly, there was too much going on to get a photo."

"That is comforting to know she was unfazed," Liv says.

"One thing we do need to talk about is future pregnancies. It's probably too early to start thinking about another baby, but I do need to mention that this was a very high-risk delivery. Another pregnancy isn't recommended. You might not be so lucky next time."

Liv wells up with tears.

"*What?* You mean, I can't have any more babies?" she sobs.

"It would be possible to extract and harvest your eggs. You could consider a surrogate to carry the baby but no, you will not be able to carry another baby to term without the risk of losing your life."

"It's okay, love. . ." I interject, rubbing Liv's hands and trying to provide any level of comfort. This is déjà vu. I'm having a flashback to the day Christine woke up in the hospital after her miscarriage. We not only lost the baby, but they had to take her uterus and ovaries out due to the cancer. *I can't believe this is happening again.*

"This is a lot of information to absorb, especially having just been through such trauma, but I need to ensure you're aware. It is imperative you take proper precautions with future birth control. Many women are still fertile even though they're nursing, so it is still possible to get pregnant. It would be extremely dangerous for both you and the baby."

"Can I still breastfeed?" Liv asks.

"Yes, if you feel strong enough to do it. You'll have to make sure you get your energy and nutrition back on track in the next day, so the milk doesn't dry up. In the meantime, we can continue to bottle feed her. She should still transition without nipple confusion."

"Okay, thank you," Liv says.

"I'll be back to check on you again tomorrow then you should be able to be released. From there, you should have a typical C-section recovery like any other patient," the doctor finishes.

The doctor closes the door behind her and Liv breaks down.

"Are you ready to trade in your lemon of a wife? How is it possible that you got not only one but *two* wives with faulty reproductive systems?"

"Liv, darling, stop. . ." I say, sitting on the bed and embracing her. "Look at this beautiful baby we made. We made her so flawless; we don't need another one."

"But I want her to have a sibling," Liv bawls.

"I grew up without a sibling and I survived. I have Mac, he's my best lad. The brother I never had. She will have two adorable, doting cousins who will always watch out for her — Livey and Owen.

I have something that might help cheer you up."

"What?" she asks.

"Close yer eyes," I instruct as I reach into my pocket for her gift and place it in her hand. "Okay, open them."

"What is it?" she asks, inspecting the jewelry.

"The lassies at the restaurant told me I had to get ye something called a 'push present.' Since you had the tough job of the delivery, I should reward you with a gift. It's a charm bracelet. I've been collecting charms in some of our favorite places. I know ye and Dan had that tradition, so I thought I would start one for us," I say as she starts to cry.

"Finn, this is so incredibly special. You are so thoughtful. How did I get lucky enough to find you?"

"The feeling is mutual, my dearest love." I kiss her as she investigates her new bling. "Let me show you the different charms. This is an Eiffel Tower, where we first professed our love for each other; then we have a journal representing your future career as a famous writer; a spoon symbolizing me and the restaurant; a dog charm for Frank; wedding bells for our glorious wedding; some maracas documenting our sexy honeymoon; a baby carriage for our sweet little Dani; and do you know what this last one is?" I ask as she takes a closer look.

"It looks like a couple of small buildings."

"No . . . it's a small town," I say as she gasps in shock then starts to cry. This time they are happy tears.

"Oh, Finn McDaniels, you overwhelm me. I love you so much."

CHAPTER FIVE
(OLIVIA)

You've never seen anyone drive slower than a new daddy driving his tiny little baby home from the hospital. I drew the line when Finn asked if he should put his hazards on along the way. He obeyed all traffic signals and made extra-long stops at all stop signs. I will admit it is surreal that Dani was inside of me a few short days ago and now we're taking her home forever. I never knew this kind of love was possible. It's like my heart is living on the outside of my body.

We get home and Finn opens the house. My parents don't get in until this afternoon. I slowly make my way out of the front seat while Finn gets the car seat. Frank is at the door, with a shoe in his mouth, waiting to greet us.

"Hi, sweet boy. I missed you so much," I say, leaning down, very gingerly, to give him some love as his turns in a circle, wagging his tail in excitement.

"Hi, buddy. Well, who do we have here, huh?" Finn says to Frank as he drops the toy from his mouth and jumps up on Finn's leg, anxious to get a closer look. He has no idea how much his world is about to change, poor guy, but I know they'll be the best of friends.

"Okay, okay. Get down, boy. Settle down. We'll let ye meet her, just give us a second." Finn walks toward the living room couch, Frank in tow.

"Liv, ye doing okay?" he asks as I move like a turtle, slow and steady. My body is still getting used to being vertical, but it feels great to be home.

"Already chopped liver. I see how this is gonna go," I quip.

"Never." He smiles and sets the car seat down on the coffee table to get Dani out. Frank can barely contain himself.

"You're home, sweet baby. What do ye think, huh?" He turns her around, showing her the room. I stop dead in my tracks. I don't think I've ever been more in love with this man than I am right in this exact moment. Seeing him holding his beautiful daughter is the sweetest thing I've ever witnessed. Things were so crazy at the hospital; it didn't really soak in. He's so comfortable with her in his arms, like she was always meant to be there. He's a natural. I'm so grateful I could give him a child. She's a lucky girl. He's going to spoil her rotten.

"Okay, Frank, *sit*," Finn says and Frank quickly obeys. He lets our pup move in a little closer to smell her. He's being so soft and gentle, and he can sense that she's something special. "This is Dani, buddy. Say hello." He keeps looking back at me to see my reaction, almost asking me if it's okay.

"He's so sweet, look at him. He's already so in love with her," I say.

Finn gets Dani settled and helps set me up on the couch. I don't want to be confined to the bedroom. My parents will be here in a little bit and I want to feel part of everything.

"Have ye given any thought to this breastfeeding thing?" Finn asks.

"Yes. I know it will be good for her, and the hospital said I can call their lactation consultants anytime. They can send someone here to work with us to make sure I'm doing it properly. I'm not going to lie; it does freak me out a little bit. What if she doesn't get enough? How am I supposed to know if it's working?"

"Welcome to parenthood, right? I don't think I've worried more in my life since the second we stepped foot in that hospital. Ye can give it a try and see if she takes to it."

"Why don't you bring her over here and I'll try."

"Ye sure you feel up to it? Last chance to bug out."

"Yes. I guess you better get used to seeing me topless," I say as he hands me the baby.

"That, my dear, is the *best* news I've heard in a loooong time."

"Ha ha." I get Dani propped in position on the pillow on my lap and put my left breast in her mouth, and she latches on.

"*Sweeeeeeet Jesus.*"

"What is it?" Finn asks.

"Are you sure she's not an anteater? Her suction has ten times the power of a vacuum, *Gooooood lord.* I don't know if she's getting any milk, but I'm pretty sure my shoulder blade is about to appear out of my nipple. I seriously don't understand how women don't talk about these things more. At least none of the women I seem to know. How have centuries of women fed their children, *multiple* children, this way? I'm pretty sure after just one day of feedings my nipples will be the consistency of hamburger meat." Finn looks at me with a 'please don't ruin your beautiful breasts' look. "I mean, just imagine having chip clips hanging off the end of each nipple. . ."

"Oy, that sounds bloody awful. Ye don't need to do this."

"You might want to get on the horn with *The Guinness Book of World Records* because I'm preeeeetty sure that is the fastest anyone has ever given up on anything," I declare.

"A Guinness sounds so good right now," Finn jokes.

"*Annnnnnd* formula it is," I reply.

My mom and dad arrive. It's true what they say about grandchildren. Grandparents will knock over anything in their path to get to them, including their own offspring.

"Let me get my hands on her," my mom says, rushing past me to reach into the bassinet, acting as if we're invisible. She scoops her hands and, in one quick motion, is holding beautiful Dani in her arms.

"Hi there, precious." She gushes along with my dad, who also gets in on the welcoming. Frank needs to get his hellos in, too. My dad is somewhat of a dog whisperer, probably because he gives them so much attention.

Once they settle in, we fill them in on the delivery scare. They are speechless and heartbroken but grateful. It was a wise decision to hold off telling them until they got here, so they can see everyone came through just fine. We all know far too well how precious time is.

I'm not going to lie; as soon as my parents arrive to the house, a calm feeling comes over me. There is no replacement for the love from your mom and dad. Now that we have Dani, I get it. I never want to let her out of my sight. I'm resolved to be a complete wreck until my dying day, worrying about her every second of every day.

My parents are experts at this baby thing. I'm so grateful they're here. We can use the help and I need to get my strength back. They dig right in. My dad starts setting up the crib. He's in charge of anything that involves lots of directions and screws, the stuff only dads tackle, and, of course, he takes Frank for a long walk. My mom begins with the baby's laundry and wastes no time getting busy in the kitchen. Finn is happy for the reprieve, so he can concentrate on his little princess, his new favorite activity. With all the commotion, I sneak off to our bedroom to take a nap as he takes Dani into her room to the rocking chair. I'm just about to dose off when I hear him start singing to her over the baby monitor.

"Go to sleep my baby/ Close your pretty eyes/ Angels up above you/ Watching very closely from the skies/ Great big moon is shining, stars begin to peep/ Time for little pickaninnies to go to sleep."

Tears start streaming down my face. That might just be the sweetest thing I've ever heard. It must be a Scottish lullaby. *Thank you, Danny for bringing Finn to me. I'm so, so grateful. He's one of a kind.*

My mom made lasagna and a nice salad for dinner. We all gather around the kitchen table and put Dani in her bouncy seat at the far end so we can all keep an eye on her.

"We need to get some nutrition in you. You've been through quite an ordeal," Mom says as she starts loading up my plate. Then I realize I'm not breastfeeding so I can have a glass of wine.

"Dad, can you pass the wine, please?" I say.

"Oh no, no, no you don't, young lady. You're not putting alcohol into your system. Not after what you've just been through."

"*Really*, Mom? Why not? I'm not breastfeeding," I huff.

"You're on pain medication so absolutely *no* alcohol. You need to regain your strength. Now that you have Dani, you should understand my position. Now eat." I guess she does have a point. I don't need any more setbacks. I haven't had alcohol in ten months and it looks so delicious.

"Thank ye for cooking, Trish. This is such a treat for me. I rarely have anyone cook for me," Finn says as he reaches for more.

"You're welcome. We promise not to get in your way while we're here. We want to help out wherever we can while Liv recovers," she says as I see my dad, not so subtly, sneaking snacks to Frank under the table. He'll never want my dad to leave. He's already had two long walks today.

"We're thrilled to have ye here. It's comforting for Liv."

"Are your folks planning a visit, Finn?"

"They don't have any set plans yet. We've been FaceTimeing, but I suspect they will get over here soon."

"Oh, I can only imagine how over the moon your parents are — first grandchild *and* a girl."

"Yes, Dani will certainly be spoiled rotten."

"Liv, did Jane tell you we went down to Austin last week to look at homes?" she asks.

"No, but that's exciting. Did you have any luck?" I ask.

"We took a few days to get familiar with the city. The only time we'd been there was for the wedding and we didn't have much time to explore. I must say, it is a lovely town with all the rolling hills and rivers. The best is the year-round outdoor living. The realtor took us around to see some places. We narrowed it down to a couple we really like. At first, we were dead set on a single-family home and resisted the senior-living concept. After they showed us the Del Webb Community, it's hard to ignore. It's located in a town called Georgetown, about thirty minutes outside of Austin. You can't argue with all the amenities they offer. Dad can play golf and not worry about yard work. I can meet some friends to play cards. Plus, I will be busy helping Jane with the twins. It just seems like much more of a community."

My dad chimes in. "You know I love mowing my own lawn and not having an association to answer to, but the extra golf will keep me busy enough."

"It sounds like you made up your mind; that's great news. Are you putting the house on the market?"

"We met with Doherty & Green Reality to get an idea of a list price and Jane is staging it as we speak. Looks like we might even make a decent profit. Our school district is one of the most desired in the Chicago area. Homes typically go within a couple days, at full price, with multiple offers. Austin has a much cheaper cost of living, so our money will go further there."

"Wow. I'm proud of you guys. I know you're not big on change, and this would be a huge one but in a positive way. Getting away from those bitterly cold winters will do wonders for you. I bet it will take years off your life. I feel like I'm a different person since moving to Palm Springs. You can live a much healthier lifestyle. People will say to you, 'but it gets so hot here in the summer.' The difference is you have nine months of mild weather versus three. It gets hot in Chicago, too. You get the worst of both extremes," I say.

"When are Jane and Peter moving?" Finn asks.

"They just put an offer in on a house this week and are in final negotiations. Peter will start in the Austin office at the beginning of the year. We're thinking: since Dani will still be so young to travel, we would all come here for the holidays. The twins are dying to meet her. It would be a fun trial run of all of our warm Christmases to come. What do you think?"

"That would be *brilliant*. Liv and I talked about wanting to start traditions now that Dani is here. Even though she'll be too little to understand, we'd love to have her first Christmas here. We'd love to have all of ye join us, wouldn't we Liv?" Finn suggests.

"Yes, I want her to grow up with her cousins. I'm not sure we have the room to host everyone here, but we'll figure it out," I add.

"Oh, we can find something on one of those vacation rental sites. Don't worry about accommodations. We just want to be together. We've never spent a birthday or holiday away from Livey and Owen, so it would only feel right to have Dani's first one be extra special."

CHAPTER SIX
(FINN)

Liv got up early this morning to do Dani's feeding. I can hear her on the monitor.

"Good morning, sweet pea. Did you sleep well? Huh? Let's get your diaper changed and we'll have some breakfast. How does that sound? Hmmm . . . Oh, oh, oh don't cry. It's coming, it's coming. I know, you're hungry. Here we go . . . there you are . . . that's what you wanted, wasn't it? Sweet baby. God, I love you so much. How did we get lucky enough to be chosen as your parents? You know Daddy and I love you to infinity and beyond. But you know who else loves you? Your guardian angels. Their names are Danny and Christine. They are very, very special. They're your godparents and their job is to always watch over you and protect you. They were Mommy and Daddy's best friends but God needed them for some special work in heaven, so they aren't here with us anymore. Maybe you were with them before you came to us . . . maybe you already know them. They love you too, very much. They were with us the day you were born, watching out for us to make sure we were okay. They will always love you, just as much as we do. See this mobile over your crib? This is what angels look like. They are white with beautiful wings. They are God's special helpers. Only the most special ones get to be with him."

As I walk around the corner to peek into Dani's room, my heart is melting. I didn't think it was possible to love this woman any more, yet every day I do. She is already an incredible mum. She's so brave and sure of herself. She hasn't complained once . . . well okay, besides the breastfeeding, but I want to keep those perky breasts all for myself so I am okay with that decision. I want the three of us to curl up in this house, like a cocoon, and never, ever leave.

It's been a revolving door of visitors. Liv's mum and da stayed with us for ten days. They are heading back home today. It's been a wonderful visit. Enough time for Liv to get some much-needed rest and they took over while I worked shifts at the restaurant. I took advantage of their time here because I knew as soon as they got on the plane, we'd be on our own with this whole parenting thing. The three of us are anxious to get into a routine and Liv is up and around much more now, regaining her strength. It's so hard for me to get up and leave them every morning. They are the best part of every minute of every day. Frank just loves Dani. He is already so protective of her. As soon as she starts crying, he runs and brings one of his toys to her to quiet her down. It's the cutest thing. Liv hired a photographer to get some newborn photos of Dani. We plan to get several photos of her and Frank together, so we can treasure these precious moments forever.

Tex has been great about my schedule at the restaurant. He's let me take whatever shifts work best until Liv feels comfortable not having me hanging around so much. Garrett's schedule is flexible enough that he can stop in when I'm not around. Tonight, Mac and Jules are bringing dinner over so they can meet Dani. She's a lucky girl. She already has so many people who adore her.

"Laddie, what's all of this?" I ask when I'm greeted by Mac with hands full of gifts, food, and wine. I reach out to ease his load.

"Just a few treats for our new niece," Mac responds.

"Yes, this is all about Dani. We picked up some Thai food. We made sure they threw in paper plates and plastic forks. We don't want Liv lifting a finger while we're here. We don't want her making any fuss over us," Jules adds.

"Well, thank ye. She's just finishing up. She'll be out in a minute." I walk them into the living room where Dani is sleeping in her bassinet with Frank lying next to it, playing watch dog.

"Oh, my goodness, how sweet is this picture?" Jules gushes.

"Ever since we got home, Frank won't leave her side. He doesn't even get up to greet people at the door. He sticks to her side and follows us around if we're holding her. And he doesn't like it when she cries. His instincts are amazing."

"Adorable." Jules peeks into the bassinet. "Oh Finn, look at *her*. She is gorgeous."

"We'll get her out after we eat. She just had a bottle so will be down for a while. We're anxious to catch up with you guys," I say as Liv appears and greets them with hugs and kisses.

"Wow, you look incredible. All rested and happy. You're already back in your regular jeans and a cute fitted top. You're making this childbirth thing look effortless," says Jules.

"Thank you," she laughs. "It's been a whirlwind that's for sure. Let's sit down to eat and we'll fill you in."

The wine starts flowing and we tell them about Liv's near-death experience. They're stunned and emotional. The memories of Christine come flooding back. Mac and Jules were there to help me pick up the pieces. The mere thought of having it happen a second time is beyond imagination for all of us, including Liv. We're so grateful for friends who treat us like their own flesh and blood. We're family to the core. We can be raw and open with them. They get it.

"Laddie, why didn't ye call us?" Mac asks.

"Things were so hectic. We were trying to process everything ourselves. Liv's folks just left. We didn't even tell them until they arrived. It turned out to be a good decision since they could see for themselves that we're all okay. We didn't want to frighten anyone. I know ye would've bent over backward if we needed ye."

"Liv, I can't imagine how exhausted you must be. If you need anything, I mean *anything*, I will drop everything and come over. I hope you know that," Jules says.

"Thank you. Believe it or not, I'm holding up well. It's been busy so I haven't spent much time dwelling on my scare, which I think is the best thing for everyone. We've been there, done that. We know Christine and Dan made sure we had a happy ending this time. It's trippy to think I died briefly though. I only wish I remembered if I saw Dan."

"Wow, you're one brave woman," Mac adds as we hear Dani squirming around. I go and pick her up. "Who wants to hold her first?" I ask.

"*Ummmmm*, me," Jules gushes and I place Dani in her arms.

"Oh my God, what a peanut. She is so beautiful. *Hi, sweetie.* I hear you gave everyone quite the scare." Jules gives Dani kisses on her forehead.

"Dani, that's Auntie Jules," I add.

"Can I be Auntie JuJu?" she inquires.

"Awww, that's so cute. I love that. JuJu it is," Liv agrees.

"Finn, have you gone back to work?" Mac asks.

"I've been picking up shifts here and there. I took advantage of her parents being here. Even though we have a lawn service, her dad insisted on doing yardwork, running errands, and walking Frank. Her mom took care of laundry, all the cooking, and did most of the middle of the night feedings so we could get some rest. It was great. Now I'm getting back to more of my normal schedule."

"Speaking of *woooork*, I have an update on yer screenplay," Mac says.

"Oh, yeah? We could certainly use some fun news," Liv replies.

"*The Man Guide* is 'green lit,' which means funding is secured and we have an official budget. The executive team is in the process of being selected: the casting director, cinematographer, and producers. I'll be the Executive Director, which means I have full creative responsibility for making yer story come to life on the big screen."

"Liv, this is *bloody fantastic!*" I say.

"Aye," Mac agrees. "I hadn't shared this previously because I didn't want to discourage ye, but there are so many instances where a screenplay gets optioned then it sits on a shelf indefinitely. Many times, it can take years to make any progress. It's a credit to ye. They love this story, Liv. I don't know if ye realize how truly talented ye are."

"Wow. This is so unexpected. I've been in mommy mode, getting ready for Dani to arrive. I buried the whole screenplay thing in the back of my mind. I'll have to wipe off the creative cobwebs to let this sink in," she says.

"They started scouting locations *annnnd* they picked Austin, Texas, to do the filming."

"No way. That is crazy. Finn, what *is* it with Austin? My sister's husband just got transferred to Austin and my parents are about to relocate there, too," Liv shares.

"That certainly *is* ironic," Mac says.

"I hate to be the wet blanket, but I do have a two-week-old baby," she says.

"Oh, no. Don't worry. Now that they've identified the location, they'll determine a shoot schedule. They are aiming for late spring next year. It'll take them time to sign the actors and get contracts in place."

"By then, Jane and my parents will be settled in Austin. Dani will be about nine months old. I guess I can stay with my family during shooting. I don't think they would object to having Dani around."

"Um, what about her Da? I'm standing right here," I interject.

"Oh, sorry, honey. How long does shooting last?" Liv asks.

"Anywhere from six to eight weeks. It isn't mandatory ye be there. I thought ye'd want to be involved in the process. This is yer dream in motion."

"I'm teasing, Liv; of course, ye will be there. We'll figure it out. At this very moment, I can't imagine having either of ye out of my sight for a second," I say.

"Aww, I can tell you're a terrific daddy already," Jules gushes.

"He is the very best. She will definitely be a daddy's girl," Liv adds, leaning over to kiss me.

"Liv, keep in mind, I will be going on location too, so I can be your nanny. We can keep Dani on-set," Jules says.

"That's a good option," Liv agrees.

"Why don't ye lassies work out the schedule? I'm thinking my best lad, and new da, needs a cigar to properly celebrate. What do ye say you, Frank, and I go out to the patio and light up?" Mac asks.

"If you can pry Frank away from his security post, I'm in," I say as we coax the pup outside. "We'll let the girls chat. Liv, why don't ye fill Jules in on the details of the breastfeeding saga."

I grab a couple beers and Mac and I get comfortable outside. It's a clear evening in the desert. The temperature is in the low seventies and the sun is starting to set. I'm realizing this is the first moment of relaxation I've had since we left for the hospital two weeks ago. Perhaps I've kept myself constantly busy so I don't dwell on the events that occurred.

"Lad, how are ye holding up? I can't *believe* ye didn't call me," Mac says.

"I'm not gonna lie; I feel like I had my own out-of-body experience. I was paralyzed with fear. Longest twenty minutes of my life. I can't imagine what I would've done if . . . "

"Don't even say the words. I can't even imagine going through it once, let alone twice," Mac says.

"It was so scary. It all happened so fast. One minute she was fine and the next minute her vitals started going crazy. Monitor alarms were going off. I knew it was serious. The doctors rushed in and swept her away. They wouldn't even let me in the operating room with her. I had to stay in the waiting room — alone. I saw that second-hand tick for the entire twenty minutes it took for them to give me an update. All I did was beg Dan and Christine to do whatever they had to do, to not take them away from me."

"Lad, I'm so sorry."

"The crazy thing is, for some reason, I sensed something bad was going to happen. I can't explain it. I had an unsettling feeling the last few months of her pregnancy. I tried to chalk it up as just being overprotective because of what I'd been through with Christine, but I couldn't shake it. I was having crazy nightmares. My intuition was right. Fortunately, it was a happy ending but unnerving."

"Maybe ye should consider going to talk to someone. Ye know? Ye have been through so much tragedy. It must weigh on ye. Ye never really took time to slow down and grieve. There is nothing to be ashamed of. I think it might help ye put it all behind ye," Mac encourages.

"I can't bear to relive it. I'd never survive."

CHAPTER SEVEN
(OLIVIA)

I'm getting back into the swing of things. Today, Dani and I are going on our first outing. We're going to visit Garrett at his store, Gin & Tonic, then stop by Christine's for Dani to meet everyone. First, I need to send an email off to the girls to give them an update.

To: Red, Liza, Alexa
From: Olivia Henry

Hi Aunties!

I'm finally coming up for air. Sorry I've not been in touch. It's been a crazy couple of weeks. My parents were here for 10 days.

Attached are some photos of the munchkin. We are SO in love with her!! She is such an easy baby. She's sleeping for 5-hour stretches — mostly because she's on formula. I gave breastfeeding a try for a hot minute. Nope, I don't think I made it a full minute before I gave it up. It's true what they say about women. As a gender, we are completely unstoppable. Me? TOTAL quitter. No way. Couldn't do it. I'll do a full demonstration when I see you. Trust me, I could sell tickets to this shit show.

I presume Jane filled you in on the scary events of the birth. We are all fine! I can't believe what I put Finn through, though — and for a second time. Breaks my heart but, despite everything, he is completely amazing! He's the sweetest daddy. He doesn't know it, but I can hear him over the baby monitor singing Dani Scottish lullabies. I want to bottle it so I can keep it forever. She's settling in perfectly and Frank is her best friend.

I can't wait for you guys to meet her! Visitors welcome!!

Love you!
XOXO

It feels good to put makeup and real clothes on. I dress Dani in her cutest outfit, a soft pink polka dot onesie with a fuchsia tutu, and off we go. First stop is Uncle Gary's shop. It's my first time driving with her and, I must say, it's nerve-racking. What's more obvious is my need to significantly clean up my road rage tendencies before Dani's first word is the F-bomb. Today, my excuse is I'm still hormonal. Garrett greets me in the parking lot to help me with the car seat and stroller. I'm still supposed to be careful about lifting things, given the surgical incision.

"Hello, gorgeous. I see you got all decked out. You look so cute," he comments.

"Aww, that's sweet. Thank you."

"I'm talking to your daughter."

"I forgot. I'm invisible now."

"You look cute, too. I haven't seen you since before"

"I know. It's okay . . . we're okay," I reassure. Garrett is not expressive but he got choked up seeing me, so I know Dani's birth was impactful. He was scared, but he was there for Finn and that means more to me than anything in the world. It will be our unspoken bond forever. We need each other. Life gives you soulmates: some are friends and one is the love of your life. Garrett is one of my soulmates. He would go to the ends of the earth for me and that's all that matters.

"Tristan can't wait to meet you so let's get you inside, princess," he gushes, rolling Dani through the parking lot.

"By the way, I've been calling you Uncle Gary. Is that okay with you, or what do you want to be called? What about GG?"

"Oh, that's cute. GG it is." We can barely get through the front door because several people are stopping to see her. I'm still a little freaked out about germs and strangers so I make it brief.

"Let's take her back to my office. Then you can get her out and don't have to worry about anyone fawning over her," he says, and I see Tristan come running from across the store.

"Oh my God. Look at her. She is a doll. Can I hold her?" Tristan asks.

"Of course. But does GG want first dibs?" I ask, getting Dani out of her car seat.

"Listen sweetie, I love her but don't get any ideas. GG doesn't do diapers. I'm better with potty-trained toddlers. I'll take her out for ice cream, her first movie, and have a slumber party. Until then, we can go shopping and you can point to whatever you want, and it's yours. I'm on board for spoiling, but I don't do babies."

"Got it," I reply.

"Perfect. More for me. Hand her over please," Tristan says. "She is so adorable. I will babysit any time. I'm great with babies."

"Deal."

"How was the visit with your parents? Sorry we never got over there. We've been down in Dana Point, working at Cotton. Plus, I thought it was probably a bit crowded and stressful." Garrett shuffles papers around on his desk. I don't know how he does it. He is in constant motion. He's managing his own business, in two different cities, and it's flourishing. He's inspiring.

"It was a nice visit. My parents were thrilled to help. You know them. They dug right in and couldn't get enough of Dani and Frank."

"Has he told you yet?" Tristan asks.

"Told me what?"

"I was going to give it a couple minutes before we dive into this being all about me. I was happy to give her five minutes," Garrett scolds.

"Listen, I've been cooped up in my house for weeks. I need some adult time, some gossip, something juicy so spill it."

"Okay, so you know the popular show *Rough Diamond* on the Home Network. They flip houses around Austin, Texas, and everyone is going mad over the cute hosts?" he begins.

"Yes."

"Welllllll, they called me and want to buy some things from Cotton and Gin & Tonic to stage in their homes." He can barely contain himself. It's the cutest thing. I haven't seen him this excited for anything in a long time.

"Oh my God! *That is huge.* How? What? When? I need all the nitty-gritty details."

"You know the couple does all their own design, research and purchasing. They found some articles on-line about me decorating the *Housewives* and other celebrities' homes. They were on a buying trip in Southern California and stopped into Cotton. They asked our store manager, Gabby, if they could talk to the owner. Of course, neither Tristan or I were in that day, so she gave them my cell phone. I guess they spent almost thirty minutes in the store, looking at fabrics and bedding. They told her they would call me directly to place the order — and they did. But the best part? In exchange for the pieces they use for staging on the show, they've offered for me to be a guest designer on an upcoming episode. I'll get air time, broader exposure, and they'll feature my items."

"That is *incredible.* I am so proud of you. When is the taping?" I say, hugging him. "Dani, did you hear that? GG is going to be famous."

"I'll have to go to Austin for a few weeks this fall for them to shoot the episode."

"This is insane. *Everything* is leading to Austin."

"What do you mean?"

"You know Jane, Peter, and the twins are moving there. They purchased a house. My parents found a place they plan to make an offer on and I found out that my screenplay, *The Man Guide,* officially got funding and will start shooting late spring — in Austin. It's nuts. Now this?"

"Let me take it one step further. Tristan and I have been tossing around the idea of opening a new store in

Austin. The area is bustling with this home show taking off. I think it's the perfect next step. Plus, I spoke to Jane. You know how she's been delving into refurbishing and painting furniture?"

"Yes."

"Well, I thought she could create a product line for the store. I could set up a workshop in the back. She can paint on-site and help run the store when we're not there. Now that I know your parents are moving there, I'll have to put your mom to work, too. This is lining up perfectly for me."

"This is so awesome. What would you name the store?"

"Luxe . . . you know, short for luxurious."

"Oh my God, I love it."

"I'd put a different spin on this store, though. It would be more shabby chic and farm style. Think shiplap, tables made from old, refurbished barn wood, and painted furniture. I'd stay true to the trends in the area."

"That's fantastic. Jane will be over the moon. She's anxious to start something like custom furniture, now that the twins are getting older. There is only one problem."

"What's that?"

"Ummm, what am I going to do in Palm Springs with all of you in Austin?"

"Tristan and I are taking a trip in a few weeks to scout locations for the store and check out real estate. We want to get another home there, too. Three is the charm, right? Three stores and three homes?"

"They say good things come in threes."

As excited as I am for Garrett, I feel this overwhelming anxiety set in. Everything is changing. I haven't really slowed down in the last couple of years, between meeting Finn, writing a manuscript, planning a wedding, and having a baby. Now Dani is here. I feel like life is starting to move at a normal pace, but everything around me is about to be uprooted. *When am I going to have a sense of calm and stillness, where I can settle in for* a while?

"We'll build a casita in the back for you, Finn, and Dani to stay in. Plus, between Jane and your parents, you'll have several options for accommodations."

"At least I'll be there for an extended stay when the film starts." I try to not let my emotions take over and concentrate on all the adventures ahead for everyone in my life.

"Yes, enough about me. Tell me. When did this all happen?"

"Mac and Jules came to meet Dani the other night. Mac shared that the movie got funding, which is a much bigger deal than I realized. He said they're lining up the producers, cinematographers, and casting director. Mac is going to be the Executive Director, which gives him control over how the story gets told."

"Do you have any say in the actors they pick?"

"Not sure. We didn't get that far. I have mommy brain. I can't wrap my head around it. Fortunately, I have several months to get my groove back."

"Liv, this is *incredible*."

"It hasn't sunk in. It doesn't feel real."

"If you get to sit in on casting calls, I will represent you as your agent. I want in."

"Okay, you can have dibs. Jules plans to come and stay with Mac on location while we're shooting, too. I'll have more babysitters than I could hope for. Right now, my biggest challenge is figuring out how we can get Finn down to Austin, so he isn't left out." Dani starts to fuss so I make a bottle.

"You're gonna have to learn to travel like a champ, sweetie. You'll be a mover and shaker. You have no idea what this life has in store for you. Nothing but good things for our princess," Garrett says, leaning into Dani to give her a kiss on the forehead.

CHAPTER EIGHT
(FINN)

Liv arrives and Dani is getting passed around like an appetizer at a fat camp. I made sure everyone washed their hands properly and stopped just shy of asking everyone to wear a facial mask. I know how many generations of new das there are out there, but it all changes when it's your offspring. I want to keep her in a bubble for the rest of her life. She is perfection. All the lassies are loving on her then I give her a tour of the place. They have a brief stay since this is Dani's first time out and about. We want to keep her in a routine as much as possible. Plus, we open in a couple hours so don't want her here with all the commotion.

"I reckon you're already a natural there, Scottie," Tex says.

"Thanks, lad. There aren't words to describe the enormity of yer love for something that little," I say.

"They are both lucky to have ya."

"That's kind of ye to say. I realized this morning that we haven't talked more about your nuptials. I know ye said you and Christie didn't want a long engagement. Have you chosen a date?" I ask.

"Funny you should mention it. I don't want to pile on more stress, but we want to get married two weeks from Monday. We want to have the reception here if that's all right with ya?"

"Of course. Whatever ye want. I've been so distracted with Liv and the baby; I hope you haven't delayed on our account," I say.

"Nah, not at all. Christie still wants to incorporate some tradition so it feels like a wedding. It's given her time to find a dress, photographer, cake, flowers, and a three-piece band to come and play here for the reception. It will be a small gathering, only about forty people. This is her day. I don't need nuthin'fancy; I just want her to be happy," he says.

"Let me know what you want the menu to be and I'll get going. And Tex, ye know this dinner is my treat. There will be no paying for *any* of this. Ye've done more than enough to help this restaurant thrive. Now it's time for ye to shine."

"That's awfully generous but I don't think"

"There's no negotiation. I don't want to hear another word. It's decided," I insist.

"Thanks, brother."

The wedding day is here. The team arrives early to prep. We want to make this as special as we can for Tex. He doesn't really have any family, so we want him to feel our love. He's a simple guy but deserves the best to start his new life off on the right foot. He's so selfless. He'd give you the shirt off your back. He's been through his fair share of tragedy, too, losing his twin brother at a young age. Those are deep scars that never leave you. They just take on a different shape.

For cocktail hour, we are serving mini crab cakes with a chili lime sauce; grilled coriander giant prawns, nested in a spicy ceviche; rosemary-roasted baby lamb

73

chops with apricot-mint salsa; mini lobster rolls on toasted brioche, and sautéed softshell crabs with a spicy rémoulade. For dinner we are serving : lobster bisque; a fried goat cheese salad with a raspberry drizzle; garlic filet, topped with a king crab leg Oscar; potato puree; and crispy Brussel sprouts cooked in a balsamic vinegar. The bakery dropped off the cake and the florist is on her way. I'm surprising them with a couple extra elements, compliments of Garrett. He hung black panels along the wall and windows to make it more formal. He added chandeliers and interspersed strings of white lights to give it more of a romantic feel. We brought in an arch and a white runner so Christie has a runway to walk down to greet Tex. They are getting married out on the patio around sunset.

Tex arrives an hour before the ceremony and is a nervous wreck.

"Ye having cold feet there, Tex?" I tease.

"I reckon it's nerves. Never done it before and ain't ever doin' it again."

"You'll be a great husband, Tex. She adores ye. I can see it in the way she looks at ye. She sees your gentle heart. Yer a good man. One of my best lads. I'm blessed to have ye as my business partner but more importantly as my friend," I say.

"I reckon as long as we're gettin' mushy, now is probably the best time to ask ya if you'll do me the honor of being my best man?"

"To use your terms— I reckon ye took my breath away. Nothing would make me prouder. I'm so happy for ya, Tex. I think we're both on the path to bigger and brighter things. We've had our fair share of pain. Time to start living. Now how about I make ye a Moscow Mule to take the edge off?"

"My favorite, perfect. Did I tell ya the story about Christie's brother?"

"Nah."

"He was staying at the house, watching the dog. Since Moscow Mules are our favorite, we keep a stash of ginger beer on hand. I reckon he drank the whole six pack, thinking it was a new beer trend. Had *no idea* it was just the mixer. He texted and asked where we got it, that he loved it but he wasn't buzzed. We had to break it to him that he consumed a few thousand calories of sugar and zero alcohol."

"*Brilliant.* I'll have to give him a hard time today when I see him. Now let's get ye married."

Tex and Christie went on a surprise honeymoon to Maui for 10 days, compliments of the restaurant staff. We all went in on the gift. They had a modest wedding and weren't planning on any trip because Tex was conscious of my schedule with Dani being so little, so it made their reaction more special. Tex hasn't ever traveled. He grew up in a small town in Texas. He's only been to New York for our show, *Delectable,* the culinary reality series where we met. Tex followed me to Vegas, then here to Palm Springs, so that's the extent of his worldliness and Christie's never left the state of California. We sprung for first-class tickets, lodging at the Grand Wailea, and sent them off with a hefty amount of cash so they wouldn't have to worry about a thing.

"How was the honeymoon? Ye look refreshed," I ask as Tex walks in while I'm prepping tonight's special, butternut squash soup and stuffed crab ravioli.

"I reckon that's what heaven is like. *Paradise*. Enjoyed every second of it." Tex shakes my hand on his way to pick up his apron, ready to dig back in.

"Glorious. That was the goal. We wanted to help start yer marriage out properly."

"Can't thank y'all enough. Trip of a lifetime, but I reckon that's the longest stretch I've ever gone not cookin'. Felt weird, like I was missin' a thumb or somethin'. So, if ya want to chase home and see Dani and Liv, I'll cover. What needs doin?" he asks, walking toward the prepping station with his utensils in hand.

"I was hoping to take advantage of the quiet and do some planning for the future."

"How's that?"

"Ye know we got fantastic reviews on the new menu at our ALS fundraisers, both here and in the Hamptons. We put expansion plans on the back burner with the baby and yer wedding, but I think we ought to start discussing. I think we should start scouting places. Follow me." I start walking toward the office, so we can have some privacy from the team. I sit down at the computer and pull up our financials.

"Our revenue has been consistent over the last two years. We average about a five-thousand-dollar profit each night we sell out, minus our costs and labor. It's added up to a significant chunk. Enough that we have a decent amount to invest in a new restaurant. I think it's time we establish some roots where you grew up in Austin."

"That'd mean a whole lot to me," Tex says. When we opened Christine's, neither of us had any ties to Palm Springs. It was almost as if we threw a dart at a map and this is where we landed. Both of us were running away from our lives in a sense, so nothing was going to feel like home, no matter where we settled. Everything has changed since then. We've both gotten married and now I have Dani. Now it doesn't matter where we go; home is where they are.

"And I haven't had a chance to fill ye in. Ye know how I told ye that Liv's entire family fell in love with Austin during the wedding weekend festivities?"

"Yeah."

"Well, as fate would have it, Liv's brother-in-law was transferred to the Austin area, so her parents decided they're relocating, too. Then Garrett was recently approached by the Home Network to go into a local partnership in the area, so now he's planning to open up a new store there."

"I reckon that right there is destiny."

"Aye. It's crazy. If I stop to think about how we ended up here, it's mind blowing. How in the world did a Scot and a Texan end up owning a restaurant in Palm Springs?"

"I reckon that sounds like the start of a bad joke — a Scot and Texan walk into a bar . . . " He chuckles.

"Aye. What do ye say? Why don't we take this freak show to Austin?"

"I believe it's already been written in the stars, partner."

"This is bloody fantastic. Ever since Dani arrived, I realize how meaningful it is to be near family. It will be important for her to grow up around her cousins and grandparents. We don't have to relocate, but we can buy a second place so Liv can fly down for spurts and split her time. I can work out a travel schedule so we both stay involved. Now to convince Liv to let me leave for a scouting trip."

CHAPTER NINE
(OLIVIA)

Time is flying by. Christmas is next week. We're going to get our first tree this weekend before Jane and my parents arrive. They rented a cute bungalow in the neighborhood for five nights so we're not all crammed in here. We have some fun things planned. We're taking Livey to the *Nutcracker*. I'm not much of a musical ballet person, so it should be interesting.

Today is Dani's six-month checkup. Her personality is starting to shine. She has a sweet demeanor. She's always happy. She only cries when she's hungry or needs her diaper changed. She's a great sleeper and is in a routine. I must admit, I do have it easy. I've slipped into mommy mode quite comfortably. We go for daily walks with Frank and I've joined a "Mommy and Me" class at the town center, so I have met some new moms. We have play groups and do a moms' night out. They are nice but they're not *my* girls. It's not that I'm not open to new girlfriends or establishing new relationships, but no one can replace the bond I have with Red, Liza, and Alexa. It's an unspoken sisterhood. We don't text like we used to. Our lives are so hectic but we need to make time. I need to plan a girls' weekend with them.

Finn is on a hike with Frank and I'm feeding Dani. She's starting solids. Little does she know her daddy is a world-class chef, so he'll never allow any mediocre food to pass through those lips. *No McDonald's for you, young lady.*

"Morning, my lovelies," Finn says, giving us both kisses.

"How was your hike?"

"Great. It's a nice morning, not too hot. What time is your appointment?"

"Ten thirty," I reply.

"I wish I could come with ye, but I have to meet with a new vendor at the restaurant. Maybe ye girls can stop by after." He gets busy in the kitchen with cooking us some bacon and eggs for breakfast. He is a hands-on daddy. He does middle-of-the-night feedings, diapers, and baths. He also does most of the laundry and makes all our meals. No complaints from me. His relationship with Dani is precious to witness. He is *so* in love with her.

"Do you want me to ask the doctor anything?" I ask.

"Do you think ye should mention how she's been waking up lately? How we hear her over the monitor and it's like she is cooing and laughing at air? It's not during tummy time when Frank is licking her. She has her moments with us, but it primarily happens when she's alone in her crib. It's the best sound on the planet, but is it a developmental concern because we're not engaging her when it happens?"

"You're just a happy girl, aren't you?" I gush, feeding her some Cheerios. "Okay, I will ask her."

Frank has become even more attentive of Dani, if that's possible, learning that random bits of food could come flying over the high-chair tray at any moment. She's crazy about him, too. She watches his every move. He doesn't even sleep in our room anymore. He sleeps in her room, as close to the crib as he can get. If he could figure out a way to get in it, he would.

"You told Tex you're taking the day off Saturday, right?"

"Aye, we're getting our first tree, wouldn't miss it." He kisses us both goodbye on his way out the door.

#

Dani gets all weighed in and measured. She is oblivious to the fact that she'll be getting pricked with shots in a few minutes, poor baby. The doctor arrives. She is a young woman in her mid-thirties. She has two kids herself so I trust her. I've had to call her a few times after hours to ask questions about Dani but she's not an alarmist, which is what I need so I don't freak out.

"Hi there, sweetie," she says, entering the room. "You've gotten big since the last time I saw you." She performs the exam and Dani is right on track with all the milestones. She can sit up, roll over, and just about pull her legs up. She's got a couple teeth coming in, but other than that she is in the right percentiles for height and weight, and healthy.

"Do you have any questions for me before I send the nurse in to give her the shots?" she asks.

"Only one, and this might sound odd so I don't want you to think I'm losing it, but over the last several weeks we've noticed that whenever she's in her crib, she starts cooing or laughing for periods of time. I mean, we've heard belly laughs, which we love, but there's nothing in her crib and not much in her room to see. We just didn't know if that was natural or if there's some sort of developmental thing we should be worrying about?"

"No, I don't think so. It's not something I've heard of before, but I'm quite sure it's just her natural behavior. I don't see anything that would make me think she would have any developmental delays. All of her motor skills are checking out and she's progressing with her milestones, so I wouldn't give it another thought. She certainly sounds like a very happy baby."

"Yes, my gynecologist told us she came out smiling," I say.

"Well, there you go, she is just one happy girl. I'll see you again in six weeks." I get her dressed and packed up in her car seat. I load her up in the car and text Finn.

LIV: Just leaving doctor's office. Asked her about our concern and she said we have nothing to worry about.

FINN: thank the Lord!

LIV: I need to get home, though; as soon as I put her in the backseat, she had an explosion so I'll see you at home tonight.

FINN: OK, love you!

LIV: Love you, too!

#

Finn gets up early and starts getting the Christmas decorations out, turns on some holiday music, and is shuffling around the kitchen, making us breakfast. He's so excited for Dani's first Christmas. We both agreed we aren't buying her any gifts because she'll be spoiled rotten by everyone else, and she has no idea what's going on. Instead, we will focus our energy on finding the perfect tree. I grew up with an artificial tree. I was the kid who wanted to have lights on our trees outside but we traveled every holiday, so my dad thought it would be a clue for would-be robbers. Finn's insistent he wants a real tree. He thinks the real pine smell adds so much spirit to the season, especially since we don't get snow. *Who can argue with that?*

We load up in the car to go to the tree farm. Dani was bathed and fed, so she should take a nap on our way. It's about a forty-minute drive. Finn wants to cut one down. No street corner Christmas tree lot for this family. We're *committed*.

"Let's take her to get her picture with Santa after this," I suggest.

"Aye. We need to start all the traditions. I thought it would be nice to get her a special ornament every year. Something meaningful that represents the year. Like this year we can get her baby booties. When she grows up and moves out, she'll have a tree's worth of ornaments."

"Aw, that's sweet but she's never moving out."

"I think we should also get ornaments that represent Danny and Christine, too. As long as we're starting traditions."

"You know what I love so much about you?" I ask.

"Apart from my stunning good looks? What?"

"Your abundant, thoughtful, and loving heart. No one would ever suspect that you're the romantic one in this relationship. It turns me to mush every single time. I love the idea."

"Does that mean I'll be getting lucky this evening, Mrs. McDaniels?"

"There is a very good chance," I say, leaning over to plant a kiss on him just long enough to tease him.

"Don't make me pull this car over, young lady," he flirts.

#

Dani is a trooper. We are out for a majority of the day and she doesn't complain once. We get home in time for dinner. We unload the car and get the tree in the stand with water.

"Why don't you get her fed, changed, and put her down for the night? I'll make us dinner," Finn offers. "We can have a fire, decorate the tree, and I can cash in on your offer from earlier."

"That sounds *fabulous*."

"I brought some crab meat home from the restaurant so I'll make us some crab cakes," he says as I get Dani loaded into the high chair.

"You, my dear, are having whatever puree is in this jar. Looks like chicken and chicken gravy, followed by some peaches. How does that sound?" I say, getting her bib on. Frank is in position.

It takes about thirty minutes to get her down after her bottle. When I return to the kitchen, Finn hands me a glass of wine.

"Go ahead and sit down. Everything is ready," he says as he serves me my five-star meal.

We enjoy our delicious meal, clean up the kitchen, and go into the family room. Finn dims the room's lights, refills my glass of wine, and turns on some Harry Connick, Jr. — the perfect holiday compilation. We start with the lights. Strands and strands of bright white lights. I don't like colored lights if you have detailed ornaments. We finish by hanging the stockings. We got one for Dani as a baby gift. We hang it on the same side of the mantle as Frank's.

"And now we're complete." He gives me a sweet kiss and a tear falls on my cheek. I'm so emotional, grateful for all my blessings. I could not ask for more. It's been a hell of a ride getting here, not that there is ever a destination, but in this moment, I'm at peace. *We made it.* We've been through hell and back, but I wouldn't trade this for *anything.*

"I have a little something for ye. It's nothing big. I know we said no presents, but I want to have a moment before your family gets here that is just ours." He hands me a small box. "It's not jewelry so set yer expectations appropriately." I open the box to find an ornament. It's a white Chuck Taylor tennis shoe. I don't even waste time with words; I just start ripping his clothes off and we make love right in front of the tree.

#

Everyone arrives safely. The twins can't contain themselves. Between Frank and Dani, they don't know what to do first.

"Okay, okay, guys. Let's sit on the couch and you can hold her, all right?"

"Me, first," Livey yells and Owen dissolves into tears. I know far too well what the younger sibling goes through. They rarely get any firsts.

"Buddy, why don't you play with Frank while Livey holds Dani then we can switch, okay?"

"Okay." He begrudgingly agrees, knowing he got the consolation prize. My mom and Jane are standing at the ready with their cameras while my dad, Finn, and Peter grab beers and go out to the patio to visit. I haven't seen Dani interact with other little kids. They all adore each other. It's endearing to watch.

Everyone gets settled into the rental and the festivities begin. We go into town for the Kris Kringle Market. The kids get candy canes while we line the street, waiting for Santa's appearance. The palm trees are strewn with white lights; there are plastic sleighs and reindeer mounted on store signs. Elves are walking around handing out candy, but none of it feels like a blustery, white Chicago Christmas.

Owen is spending the day with the guys and Dani while my mom, Jane, and I take Livey to her first musical. She is excited because she doesn't know what to expect. The doors open and we shuffle into the theater with the rest of the crowd and find our seats. It's an old theatre with the uncomfortable red chairs an inch from your neighbor. My mom sprung for the good seats so we could get the full experience. The lights dim, the show begins, and the actors take the stage. I look over at Livey in her pretty little green Christmas dress, black tights, and fancy black shoes, wide eyes soaking it all in. I don't even think she blinked for the first two minutes. I'm so glad she is enjoying it. Intermission arrives so we stretch our legs and go out to the concession area. We get some popcorn and candy and chat for a few minutes. The lights flicker so we go back to our seats and get situated. The curtain rises and the ballerinas come back out on stage to the classic *Nutcracker* theme song, and all I hear is Livey say, "Oh no, not again." My sentiments *exactly*. This is *boring*. Ballet and opera is *not* my thing.

CHAPTER TEN
(FINN)

"Good morning, love," I say, snuggling Liv in bed before the baby wakes up.

"Mm, as much as I am dying for more sleep, I never grow tired of you wanting me," she replies.

"Let's take a shower before Dani wakes up," I say, pulling the blankets off her.

"If you insist," I lead her into the bathroom, turn on the water, and we climb in. I start by washing her hair then lathering up her body, which leads to amazing, hot, and steamy sex. I love touching her. She isn't the slightest bit self-conscious about her body, even since she had the baby, nor should she be. She's confident. She knows I love every inch of her no matter what. She brought the best thing in our lives into this world with her beautiful body. *How could I not treasure it forever?* She is perfect just the way she is.

I finish brushing my teeth while Liv gets dressed for the day. She puts on a pair of white shorts and a light blue t-shirt that hugs her body perfectly. I wrap my arms around her waist from behind and kiss the back of her neck.

"Yer one hot mum, ye know that?" I compliment.

"Thank you for always making me feel beautiful. Do you know how much I love you?"

"I think I have an idea." It's important to me that we always make time for each other. We both make our marriage a priority. We steal private, intimate moments whenever we can. She's my best friend. I need her not only emotionally but physically. Our connection is one of the things I treasure the most. I'll never take her for granted.

"Ye know how Tex and I talked about expanding?" I ask.

"Yes."

"I think we're ready to start scouting locations."

"Really? That's super exciting."

"We've looked at the financials and now is as good a time as any. We have the capital to do it. We've done our research and the food is different enough that we won't be saturating the market. Our menu was a hit at the fundraisers, so we've piloted the concept. I don't think it will be hard to differentiate ourselves in Austin, and we all know that Tex is the king of Tex-Mex BBQ. I want this for him. Something he can always go home to."

"I support you one hundred percent. I think there's no better time than the present. Recently, you've gotten all those magazine and blogger write-ups praising Christine's. There is a wait list at least a couple deep for reservations. Now is the time," she says.

"The craziest thing is how our lives intersected and now we're all on a path leading to — Austin."

"It's fate. How would we handle restaurants in both locations? Would we get a place in Austin?"

"Tex and I still need to sort out the details but that is the thought. We can get a second home in Austin so we can be near yer family. It's important for Dani to grow up with her cousins and grandparents. Tex and I don't have any real ties here in Palm Springs, outside of the restaurant. Would it make you sad to leave here?" I ask.

"No, I don't really have any strong attachments here. Home is wherever you and Dani are. I would love for her to grow up with her cousins since she doesn't have siblings. You see how close Garrett and I are. It's a special bond that I would love her to have. There is a bit of an age gap now, but they'll grow into it. You saw how sweet they all were together over the holidays. It's almost like Dani is the twins' third sibling."

"Agreed. Family is everything. I'm anxious for my folks to get here so they can meet Dani."

"Do you think they would consider moving to the States?" Liv is putting her makeup on when we hear Dani stir over the monitor.

"Ask me after my mum lays her eyes on her in a couple days," I say as we get Dani out of her crib.

"You sure are irresistible, that's for sure," Liv says, smothering our daughter in kisses.

#

No matter how much Tex and I come and go around Christine's, our team stays consistent. They deliver quality food and impeccable client service, every single day. We take great pride in the staff we retain. Retain being the key word. We want everyone we hire to feel like our family, to be invested. It took us a long time to find the right mixture of people. It's more than skill; it's a culture and dynamic we want to maintain. Christine's should perform at the same level, no matter who you are or when you dine. Even though Tex and I have some national recognition, we can't ever get lazy. There are always people trying to be bigger and better. We must stay at the top of our game, be fresh, and infuse greatness into every aspect of the experience here. This is the dream we've built; we'll never take it for granted. We take care of our staff. We like to switch things up. We let them choose daily specials on occasion to keep things fresh. They all have the authority to reject any meal that comes off the line if they don't feel it's up to standards. It keeps everyone on their toes. We run contests. We give out random bonuses. We want our team to feel valued and appreciated by recognizing their unique talent. It requires each piece of the puzzle to be successful.

Today starts out like any other day at the restaurant. Tex and I are in the galley, prepping.

"I spoke to Liv about the expansion this morning and she is onboard," I say.

"I spoke to Christie about it. I reckon she ain't as keen. She don't like change. She's grown up here her whole life. This is all she knows," Tex says.

"Tex, I just thought of this, and I think it's the perfect solution," I say.

"What's that?"

"Yer establishing roots here. Liv's whole family is moving to Texas. It's like our lives are interchanging. What if we worked out a plan where ye can stay here and run the day to day, and I will assume management over the new restaurant? We would still be equal partners in both."

"That ain't a bad idea," Tex says.

"I want us to find a way to incorporate Liv and Christie into this dream. Our journeys led us both here to them. What if we surprise your wife with an official dedication ceremony and I'll hand over the reins here. There's only one stipulation."

"Depends on what it is."

"I get to name the new place."

"Deal."

"Let's keep all of this under wraps until it's more formalized. We'll tell the lassies that we're moving forward. We won't share any specifics until the time is right. Keep them both in suspense."

"I ain't gonna argue with that. Now finish making that balsamic reduction for our lamb chop special, " he quips, as we shake on it.

#

We're about two hours into dinner service when our hostess, Maddie, enters the kitchen in a flurry.

"What is it?" I ask. My only guess is we have an unhappy customer on our hands, which is rare.

"I just sat a table of two men in suits. I kept my eye on them for a couple minutes to ensure they were approached in a timely fashion. They look like they would complain about the smallest mistake. Ryan is waiting on them. I met him at the bar when he placed their drink orders, and he told me to come back here and tell you he thinks they are Michelin star inspectors," she says. "I don't know what that means but he seems nervous."

Tex overhears her and we look at each other in complete disbelief. A Michelin star has never been on our radar. Chefs prepare their entire careers for a moment like this. We've never prepped the team or performed any simulation for how we would respond. I guess it shouldn't be a shock. We're in Northern California, which is an eligible region to be considered for a star and we have been getting a lot of publicity as of late. It just never crossed our minds.

"I reckon I ain't ever expected nothing like this." Tex runs his hands through his hair.

"Me neither. As far as we're concerned, this is just like any other night. We don't want to stress out the staff. We're just going for it," I respond.

Christine, I'm calling in a last-minute favor. Help us do what we do best. I don't want to show my cards to Tex, so trying to play it cool. Having a Michelin star would mean the world to both of us. It would prove that everything we've poured our hearts into has all been worth it. It would be the icing on the cake. Oh, and I didn't run it past you before I blurted out handing over the restaurant to Tex. I hope you're okay with him making it his own. I know you would agree it's time to move on. You'll be with me no matter where I go. I know you know that.

"Couldn't agree more,' Tex agrees. We round up the team for a quick pep talk, which isn't unusual.

"Ye know Tex and I think yer the best team around. We're proud of each one of ye. Keep up the amazing work. Let's give everything a little extra TLC before it goes out those doors tonight. Okay?" I announce and the team responds with a cheer.

The assumed inspectors order the menu favorites. Their job is to review everything. They evaluate décor and location, cuisine and cocktail flavoring, customer service and overall experience. The stars are awarded in levels:

One star —A very good restaurant in its category

Two stars —Excellent cooking, worth a detour

Three stars —Exceptional cuisine, worth a special journey

The entire system is secretive. No one knows what the criteria is, when or where the selection process happens, or what the inspectors look like. They are all anonymous. Even if we think we are being considered, we would never know until the guide is published, which won't be for months. Sometimes, inspectors make several visits before they make a final decision so this could be the first of many, or perhaps we'll be eliminated. Either way, Tex and I have faith in the staff so no matter what happens, it was meant to be.

I get home late from the restaurant. Liv picked up my mum and da this afternoon but they are resting now from the jet lag. She pours us some wine and we lay on the couch to catch up on our day. I fill her in on the potential Michelin Star craziness at Christine's and she tells me how much my parents fawned over Dani. They informed Liv they want to be called Nan and Pop. It's adorable that they've already thought about it when Dani is probably a year away from her first word. Liv has several plans in store for them. They've never been to the States. They are staying for two weeks since it is such a long trip. It's a good mixture of sight-seeing and grandbaby activity. They plan to go to the zoo and attend one of Dani's Mommy and Me classes. They'll, of course, have a couple meals at Christine's. My parents aren't big outdoorsy people so nothing too active. There won't be any hikes, just walks with the stroller and Frank around the neighborhood. They want to see our world and be a part of our lives here, but the most important thing is to spend quality time with Dani.

"Is now a good time to tell ye my surprise?" I say.

"Surprise? What on *earth*"

"I want to give my mum and da some special Dani time so I may have booked us a three-day, two-night trip up to Napa."

"We're leaving your parents with our newborn?" she responds.

"She's almost seven months old. Hardly a newborn. And ye might forget but my mum is a mum. I think they will be fine. Plus, I think they'll be thrilled to have her to themselves. I told Garrett so they will be on call."

"Well, you did go to all the trouble, so I guess we can go," she says in a flirty tone.

"I thought I'd take advantage of having live-in babysitters for a few days. I don't want us to be defined *just* as Dani's parents now. It's important to me that we keep our own relationship. We're technically still newlyweds. We're both so busy and before you know it, you'll be on a movie set and I'll be traveling back and forth scouting restaurants. I still want you to myself. Is that selfish of me?"

"If your parents weren't sleeping in the next room, I would take your pants off and have my way with you right here," she says playfully.

"How about we make our way to the bedroom and ye can do whatever ye want with me."

Chapter Eleven
(OLIVIA)

Finn's parents left a few days ago and now my girls are coming out to visit this weekend. There is something about hanging out with your girlfriends that takes you back to a time of innocence and freedom. Life's chosen sisters. They're your safe place. They'll carry you when you're broken and be the biggest cheerleaders waiting for you at the finish line. It's important to nourish relationships outside of your marriage. You were your own person before you met. You can't lose that piece of yourself when you're in a partnership. If you're with the right mate, they will only encourage you to foster those friendships. It's rejuvenating. Girlfriends fill a different part of the heart. They make it overflow with goodness. Danny was in that category, and I miss him more than words can describe, but I'm grateful for these women. They are some of the best parts of me. Their love and encouragement have catapulted me past any dream I could have accomplished on my own. Each of them is a unique treasure.

Red: Are you picking us up at the airport or should we get an Uber to the house?

Olivia: Dani and I will be curbside to pick up all her aunties!

Liza: Can't wait to get there!

Alexa: I call first dibs with Dani!

Olivia: I can't wait to see your faces. Dani is excited, too. She's heard so much about all of you.

Red: See you soon! XO

Olivia: Love you! Travel safe! XOXO

I see them exit the baggage claim doors amongst a sea of people and can barely contain myself. I start honking to get their attention and wave like a crazy person. I hop out of the car and greet them all with bear hugs as we load up their luggage and they fight about who gets to sit next to Dani in the back seat.

"I'm pretty sure Alexa called it," I laugh.

"We can't wait to get ahold of her," Liza says.

"Hands off ladies, I've known Liv the longest so I clearly get the first snuggle," Red chimes in.

We gab and laugh the whole way home. I point out the scenic mountain views along the way. We arrive at the house and I give the girls a tour and show them to their rooms. We have four bedrooms: the master, the nursery, and two luxurious guest suites. Of course, Garrett put his stamp on the house after we got married. One guest bedroom is Ralph Lauren themed. It has navy walls with muted florals and striped bedding, covering a king-size bed. The other bedroom is part home office and part desert oasis. It has khaki linen wallpaper with crisp white bedding on a queen bed. A large, black modern desk, where I do my writing, overlooks the pool. Both rooms have full, spa-inspired bathrooms. Alexa and Liza take the king room to share and Red makes herself comfortable in the other room.

"Liv, come here for a second. We have a surprise." Red calls us to her room. Liza and Alexa claim a spot on the bed as Red hands me a gift.

"What is this? I told you there will be no spoiling of Dani. That is not what this trip is about. She just wants to meet her aunties," I say when Red interrupts.

"It's not what you think. You'll see. Just open it." I hand Dani over to Liza while I unwrap the package. I open the lid and remove the delicate tissue paper to uncover a sweet, stuffed, medium-sized, brown teddy bear. It's a little battered. The left ear is ripped, he has a crooked eye, his nose is hanging on by a thread, and the red ribbon around his neck is frayed.

"This is *cuuuuuute*. Couldn't spring for a new one?" I joke.

"You'll soon regret that statement." She laughs. "I ran into Mrs. Sullivan. She got your baby announcement and asked me to stop by the house to bring you a gift. She found it packed away in a box when they were cleaning out Danny's stuff. She was saving it to give to him when he had kids. It was his favorite childhood stuffed animal. He got it from his godmother when he was born. She said he never sucked his thumb or had a pacifier, but he never was without Teddy. That's what he called him."

"Aww, really?" Tears stream down my cheeks.

"She said he looks tattered but he's been re-stuffed twice and his head has been sewn on at least four times, but he's sturdy and she wants your Dani to have him."

"That is the sweetest thing ever," Alexa says.

"*Dani*, look what we got. He is super special. This is from your godfather, Danny, the one we tell you about all the time." I pick her back up, handing her Teddy. "I'm overwhelmed. Thank you so much. This is the best. He *still* leaves me speechless. We will treasure it, won't we sweetie?"

"Did you stock up on tissues? I have a feeling this weekend is going to be a doozy," Liza says.

"We will *not* be sobbing all weekend. I do have some fun activities planned. I promise. First on the agenda is a hike," I announce. We change and fill up our water bottles to stay hydrated. I strap Dani into her backpack, we grab Frank, and we're on our way. We're so fortunate to have access to great trails right outside our backdoor.

Finn is waiting for us when we get back. He came home early to take over daddy duty. The wine and prosecco start flowing and we continue the party by cooling off in our pool while Finn grills us a delicious steak dinner. Dani loves the water. She's floating around in her inflatable duck. She is just happy to be a part of all the action. She is very social.

I must admit, it's amazing having a chef for a husband. It makes entertaining a piece of cake. He takes care of all the meal planning, shopping, cooking, and knows how to make every cocktail under the sun. We have a cleaning lady so there is nothing left for me to do. I am completely off the hook. I just need to make sure Dani and I are dressed and ready to go.

Finn has a fresh spread awaiting us when we wake up. He's made gourmet egg puffs, stuffed with bacon and goat cheese; a platter full of fruit; freshly squeezed orange juice; and mini French toast sticks for the ladies who like their sweets in the morning. Dani is awake and chatty as ever. She has such a great disposition. I'm glad the girls get to enjoy her at this stage. She is starting to come into her personality and is more engaging every day. After we eat, the girls lay on the living room floor all around her, playing with her and handing her toys. She is laughing and giggling. Frank wants in on the action, too.

"Do you see that hand gesture she keeps making?" I ask. "She does it all the time and I have no idea what she's doing."

"The motion she's making is sign language for 'more.' You can teach babies some basic sign language, as early as six months, for common things like milk, more," Liza responds. "And she's using it in the right context. Watch. See when I play peek-a-boo then stop, she gestures because she wants me to do more."

"I had *no idea*," I say.

"Babies' cognitive skills are much stronger than their ability to communicate. It helps to reduce frustration and breaks down the communication barrier so when they are fussy you can try to understand what they want," Liza explains.

"Neither Finn or I have ever used sign language around her, so how did she learn it? She isn't with anyone else but us." I'm surprised by Liza's information.

"That is *strange*. Maybe she's a genius, *aren't you?*" Alexa chimes in, rubbing Dani's belly.

"Now my head is spinning. I'm starting to piece together other oddities we've witnessed." I pause. "Sometimes, when we go into Dani's room to get her out of her crib, we'll see a stuffed animal or a toy laying on the floor that *we know* was put away. We never gave it much thought. We assumed Frank got ahold of it. I mean, it's almost like they have their own language. Now that I'm thinking about it, I've only ever seen him bring *his* toys over to her. I've *never* seen him with anything of hers in his mouth."

Finn overhears the conversation and steps into the room as I'm finishing my thought.

"Ye don't think. . ." he starts.

"Think *whaaaaat?*"

"That we might have a couple of suspicious angels involved?" he says.

"That is *insane*. I am the biggest believer there is, but even *I think* that's crazy talk. They communicate through signs and symbols. They don't have the ability to touch or move things. No, *no*. *That's* where I draw the line."

"Ye never know, maybe Dani's broken through the next barrier," he says. "Maybe we only get signs and symbols and the next generation goes a layer deeper." He sees the shock and disbelief on my face. "I can't believe yer the cynic in this scenario." The girls all look at me as if they agree with Finn.

"This is crazy talk, *right?* You guys agree with me, don't you?" I ask.

"I don't put anything past Dan but I can't speak for Christine. I never met her," Red admits.

"Okay, on that note, I think that's our cue to head out. Our appointments are in ninety minutes and I don't want us to feel rushed." I need to break up the moment. For whatever reason, I'm uncomfortable with this conversation. *But why? How amazing would it be if our angels are co*-existing in our physical world but we can't see *them?* I admit I can feel Danny around on occasion. I get a chill or feel a breeze but I've never heard of an angel that can physically move things. That's *next level*. I'm not sure I could even be convinced of that. We all pile into the car and while everyone is getting situated, my mind drifts off for a moment.

Danny, this is ca-rrrra-zy, right? I mean, I love you more than anything. Knowing you can see, watch over, and protect me is comforting, but this might be too much. Wait, she is always laughing and smiling at nothing. We hear her giggling and babbling over the monitor all the time. Now she's learned to sign. Did YOU teach her how to sign? Can Dani actually . . . see you? No, no, this is too much. Okay, here is the ultimate test. You need to send me an undeniable sign, something that will blow my mind, something there's no way to dispute, to prove to me that she CAN see you. I won't time box it. I'll let you surprise me. No, overwhelm me.

We arrive at the spa, which is built into a vast mountain side on old Indian tribal grounds within Palm Springs. It's known for its natural hot springs. It has seven different outdoor mineral pools so the setting alone makes you feel one with nature. They all have varying temperatures, each labeled with a spiritual name and the contents enhance inner healing: removing stress, detoxing, or infusing minerals. It's a very peaceful and tranquil setting. There are signs posted everywhere indicating it's a quiet zone so guests can enjoy the experience. We have time before our massages so we get changed and make our way out to start our day of relaxation. We hit the Kinoa Pool first, which concentrates on overall digestive health. We're getting settled in when Alexa whips out a bathing cap like she'll be performing a synchronized swimming routine on command. We all explode into hysterics. The quintessential inappropriate church laugh. The kind that gets worse the more you try to avoid it. We haven't been here for ninety seconds and we're already causing a scene. *Perfect.*

"What?" Alex asks. "I don't want to get my hair wet. They're pools. People splash."

Alexa has a hair condition. By that, I mean she has a lot of it and needs to have it managed professionally. She receives a keratin chemical treatment a few times a year to take the bulk and frizz out of it. In addition, she gets it blown out, by a stylist, twice a week. She isn't someone I would ever consider to be high maintenance. I'm immune to it since I lived it throughout our college years. I just forget these dramatic precautionary measures, so it makes this moment even more entertaining.

On the way home, we stop at Gin & Tonic to see Garrett. The girls have been dying to see his store. Red is in the middle of a home renovation and wants to get some design advice. She brought some colors and fabric swatches to show him. A little free consultation, for friends and family, is allowed on occasion.

"Ladies. Welcome," Garrett states. "You all look refreshed. Fill me in on all the fun that's happening."

"We're on our way back from the Advika Spa. We've been rubbed, massaged, covered in mud, and soaked in every hole in the ground within sixty square miles of here," I reply.

"Sounds heavenly. Why wasn't I invited?"

"Girls only," Alexa jokes.

"Like I said, why wasn't I included?" Garrett giggles.

"Well, we're here now," I say. "They're all yours."

"Let me show you ladies around."

He leads them on a tour through the store. They are soaking in every detail. They've seen his website, but it's very different when you experience his genius in person. You can touch the fabrics and see the quality and different layers with accessories. Red corners Garrett to gather his input and I hear him making some suggestions and improvements.

"So, tell us all about your new venture," Alexa says.

"Well, we just signed a long-term lease on a store front in the South Congress neighborhood in Austin. It'll be a different vibe than this. Different demographic. More southern, shabby chic meets cowboy. We're super excited."

"Liv filled us in on the cameo on *Rough Diamond*. That is amazing," Alexa says.

"I can't believe this will be our third store. Never in our wildest dreams did we see this level of expansion. It's crazy. We open later this spring. Our little movie star should be knee deep in filming," he says, hugging me.

"I know, the next time we see you might be on the red carpet at the movie premiere," Liza adds.

"Indeed. So many exciting things happening for all of us."

"Next stop is Christine's for dinner. Nothing but the best for my besties," I say as Red finishes paying for some serious purchases.

Her order is just shy of eight-grand. Garrett has an ability to drain people of their money and secrets.

#

We're seated at the best table in the house, of course. Finn is home with Dani, so Tex makes sure to give us the royal treatment. He personally serves us small plates of most of the appetizers and entrees, as the bottles of wine are flowing.

"We've waited as long as we can. Spill it. When do you leave for Austin?" Red asks.

"In a little less than six weeks. Believe it or not, I haven't given it a ton of thought. With Dani, I tend to live more day to day, more like hour to hour. My parents and Jane have settled into their new houses. Jane lives in Westlake and my parents are about thirty-five miles outside the city in a fifty-five- and-older community. Garrett is looking in an area called East Austin. I will have lots of choices for lodging and Dani will have her choice of babysitters. I rented an Airbnb for two months for nights we are shooting late and I want to stay closer to set. We'll be all over town so I found something central. Finn will be traveling back and forth, too, because they are scouting new locations."

"Liv, wow. All the Henrys and McDaniels are on fire," Alexa says.

"It's crazy but wonderful. We're counting our blessings."

"I love all these updates but, let's be honest, we want the real dirt. Who are they casting in the movie?" Liza asks.

"You suuuuure you're ready for this? I can hardly believe it myself *but* Jack McNichols and Chloe Armstrong," I answer.

"*Whhhaaaaattttt?* They are both serious A-listers. How did they land them? That's incredible."

"A- or B+ listers but yes, it's pretty huge. I cannot believe that Chloe Armstrong will be playing a character based on my life. Never in my wildest dreams. . ."

Red clears her throat. "Excuse me, but I better get a 'day in the life' on set with you since I'm responsible for getting you to Second City."

"Cheers to that." Alexa raises her glass in a toast. "Wait, no, we need champagne for this." She gestures for Ryan to get us a bottle.

We end up staying until close. Tex orders an Uber to get us home safe.

CHAPTER TWELVE
(FINN)

"I don't say it enough but I am so proud of you. Incredibly proud," Liv says.

I'm flying to Austin for three days to scout locations for our next restaurant. I hate leaving my girls. No one ever tells you this part. The part where you only feel whole when you're all together.

"It's just a few short days but I'll miss ye," I say.

"Go find our next Michelin star. Say bye to Daddy," Liv says. I smother them both in kisses while they stand at the end of the driveway. I can see them waving goodbye in my rearview mirror as I drive up the street.

Tex hooked me up with a local commercial broker who has some places earmarked for us to look at. We don't have an exact city or town to concentrate on. We're leaving the search area open, so the realtor has places lined up within a sixty-mile radius. The decision will be made based on a feeling. That's how we found Christine's. I'm not sure exactly what I'm looking for, but I'm confident I'll know it when I see it. Tex is letting me take the lead. We know each other well enough; we trust each other. He's always made it clear that he prefers to work in the background. He doesn't like all the fuss upfront. He's more of a roll up your sleeves and get to work kind of lad.

Liv's dad is picking me up from the airport. I'll be staying with her parents while I'm here. Dick and

Jane's husband, Peter, are going to accompany me on the search. They both bought new homes and are familiar with and enjoy the process. I'd love their opinion. Peter's hobby is to tear down and flip homes. His goal is to retire early and start a second career as a quasi-builder. He can provide context on the structure and the quality of the land. He has knowledge of the surrounding neighborhoods.

"Finn, how are you? I'm your personal You-ber," Dick says as he reaches in for a hug. He's waiting for me outside security. I can't tell you the last time I had someone park their car and pick me up inside the airport. It's engrained in his generation. They lived a slower paced life. I remember my folks used to have friends stop by all the time just to visit. People didn't talk on the phone. If they wanted to see their friends, they had to physically go see them. I don't think today's generation understand how lucky they are to be so connected all the time. They need to learn to use it the way it was intended.

"Glorious. Thanks for picking me up." I laugh.

"Wouldn't have it any other way. We're going to pick up Peter then we can meet with the realtor."

"Brilliant. Do you want to say hello to your granddaughter?" I ask as we approach his car in the parking garage.

"I would love nothing more. Is she packed away in your suitcase?" he responds. Dick's a character. He's got a quick wit.

"Nah, I'm going to FaceTime Liv to let her know I arrived safely. Dani should be getting up from her nap."

"Get them on the horn."

Liv answers and is holding Dani.

"Say hiiii Daddy. Hiiii Grandpa." It takes a second but Dani is starting to grasp the concept of FaceTime. She recognizes us and keeps reaching for the phone. "Show Grandpa what you learned. Dad, start waving to her," Liv instructs. Within a few seconds, Dani starts to wave. It's her latest milestone and the cutest thing *ever*.

"Aww. Hi, sweet dolly. Grandpa loves you." He starts waving and making all sorts of faces and blowing her kisses. Then we hear her say, "Dada."

"Did she just say what I think she said?" I ask.

"Aww, she did. She's never said it before. She must really miss you, Daddy. Hurry up and get home to us," Liv says.

I well up with tears. There is nothing more precious than hearing those words come out of your baby's mouth. Each new milestone is better than the last. This is the best use of technology. A granddad making your daughter laugh then hearing her say da for the first time, thousands of miles away, is priceless.

My broker, Tiffany, meets us and we get through the first three options quickly. One was in a strip mall, one was in the middle of nowhere, and the third wasn't big enough. I'm looking for something old and rustic. I don't know why but when I think of BBQ, I think of a grittier environment. Somewhere you can get your hands dirty and not worry about getting sauce everywhere. We're approaching the last stop of the day. It's out in the country and not far from Tex's ranch in Dripping Springs. The land is flat but expansive. You can see rolling hills off in the distance. We drive up a long, dirt road onto the property.

"I saved this property for last for a reason. You'll have to think outside the box on this one. Tex told me you got married on his ranch, so I know you're familiar with his land. This is similar. It's unique and you could make it an experience. Please bear with me and keep an open mind, but we need to make a quick decision. This will be going on the market tomorrow. It's been in this family for five generations. Miss Mary Barrington was ninety-six when she passed away. She lived here her entire life. She didn't have any kids of her own so her niece and nephew inherited the estate. They are heartbroken at the thought of selling but there isn't anyone who lives locally to take care of the property. The family has been approached by investors wanting to buy the land. They'll turn this into a subdivision, office park, or commercial outlet. I told them you were coming and that I had an idea in mind so they're waiting to entertain bids until they hear back from me. I thought, at a minimum, maybe you'd buy the land and build a restaurant on it. They would feel so much better knowing the land would go to a local like Tex. They like the thought of keeping some history around it." She pulls up to the farm house. "They sold off the cattle and livestock about twenty-five years ago so it hasn't been a working farm in years, but the bones are here. It's in desperate need of some TLC. Anyway, you guys go ahead and look around and let me know if it sparks any interest. One last ditch effort for the Barringtons."

Christine, give me a sign when I've found it but so far, this looks promising.

It's an overcast day, mist falling lightly. We get out of the car and start walking the property. The grounds are reminiscent of the wedding venue. There are rows of lush green trees and purple wildflowers covering the fields. It's picturesque. The land has three large lakes.

Dick can come take Dani fishing here, which they'll both love.

"This might sound bloody crazy but I have the perfect vision," I say as I stop dead in my tracks in front of the barn. Through the light drizzle, the sun pierces through a small crack in the scattered clouds to illuminate the brightest rainbow.

"What's wrong?" Dick asks, seeing the stunned look on my face.

"Nah, nothing. Before I go there, Peter: do you think the house and barn are structures that can be salvaged?"

"I mean, they're old but you *could* reinforce and bring everything up to code. It would all need a major overhaul but you could work with it. Depends on how much you're willing to spend. Anything can be accomplished for a price," Peter says.

"I'm thinking we buy the land and keep the existing buildings intact. The farm house has ten bedrooms and we turn it into a bed and breakfast. I can have chickens so we can serve fresh eggs to our guests every morning for breakfast. Farm-to-table concept. We turn the barn into the restaurant. There's enough separation on the acreage to make them feel independent. Plenty of space to build a parking lot. We can set up an outdoor area with fire pits and picnic tables. Enclose some of it where we can have live music while they wait. Maybe we can even invest in our own livestock. We could keep them at Tex's ranch," I suggest.

"That is an awesome idea. It's going to cost you though. I'd say you need to count on at least a million," Peter says.

"I'm not done yet. I'd want you to build Liv, Dani, and I our dream house farther back on the property."

"You're planning to relocate here?" Dick asks.

"I'm keeping all of this a secret from Liv, so you can't tell Trish or Jane. They'd never be able to keep it to themselves, and this is going to take months to bring to fruition. When Tex and I spoke about expanding, he mentioned his wife Christie isn't interested in splitting her time between California and Texas. It would be a lot for both of us to travel back and forth, so we agreed that Tex will take over full control of Christine's, and I would take responsibility for the new restaurant. With all of you living here now, it makes sense. Liv and I don't have any ties to Palm Springs. We want Dani to grow up with her cousins and grandparents. It's all that matters." Dick turns and walks away because I can tell he is getting emotional. There is nothing more important than family.

"That's incredible, man," Peter says, hugging me. "Welcome home."

"Aye. This feels right. I think we can make it something special. How do you feel about building a restaurant?"

"I'm up for the challenge. This would be an amazing project. It might even be the linchpin that forces me into retirement," he comments.

"Bloody fantastic. We only need one more blessing," I say as I FaceTime Garrett.

"That looks like trouble," he answers. "What's going on?"

"How quickly can you get on a plane and come down to Texas? We need your help." I pitch him our concept.

"I'm already getting in my car. I'll call you when I land. Finn, your job is to negotiate the best deal you can so you leave us with the biggest part of the budget." He grins at me.

"Done."

I call Tex and run through the whole scenario to get his approval. He loves the idea, including the cattle and is 100 percent on board. We agree to an offer price. I'll be paying a much larger percentage, of course. This will be incredible. I never dreamed of owning a bed and breakfast but we can make it a family project. Dick and Trish are still young at heart and have plenty of energy to help run this place. We just want the best for Dani. This would be an incredible place for her to grow up. She can learn the value of hard work and we can leave her and the twins a legacy. This can be our family's stamp on history. *Who knows?* Maybe it will get passed down five generations with stories to tell for centuries to come.

We meet back up with Tiffany at the car and climb in.

"Well, what do you think besides me being crazy?" she asks.

"It's bloody perfect. How much are they listing it for?" I ask.

"Really? Wow, that is amazing. They're planning to list it for one million five-hundred thousand," she says.

"That's what I assumed. Do ye think we can convince them to come down if we tell them we plan to refurbish everything that's here?"

"Heavens. I never dreamed you'd keep it. I assumed you'd bull doze it, keep it for the land, and build your own restaurant."

I fill her in on the vision as we drive to lunch. I'm anxious to tour the area to see what's around. Peter said it's a very up-and-coming area. In the next five years, this will all be developed land, so the timing is perfect to scoop it up while prices are still somewhat reasonable. Land will double in price by then.

"What if we go in at a million two hundred and fifty thousand and see if they bite? I really don't want to go any higher than that. We'll have to put the same amount into renovations to turn it into what we want so that would be my best and final offer," I say.

"Okay, y'all go in and get a table while I call the sellers," she says as we arrive at a trendy wood-fire pizza joint.

"How do you plan to keep this from Liv?" Dick asks.

"She knows we're expanding so she's expecting a new restaurant. The surprise will be the bed and breakfast and the new house. She doesn't know we're permanently relocating. She'll be distracted with filming the movie so I don't think it will be hard to keep her away. I'll still be traveling back and forth so I can position it carefully. I'll tell Liv I want her to get the full experience, so I don't want her to see it until it's all done. I won't make a big deal out of it. She'll respect my wishes. Tex and I didn't tell either of the girls our plan. We want it to be special. I can share that Peter is helping. There will be just enough discussion around it that it will keep Liv off the scent." I see Tiffany walking back to the table and can't read the expression on her face. I hold my breath.

"Well, it's all yours!" she says.

"That is bloody fantastic. Thank ye. You just changed our lives forever in the best way possible."

#

We pick Garrett up and the four of us go back out to the property. He needs to see all the nitty-gritty details so he can start his planning.

"Do you think Liv will get mad at you for not including her?" Peter asks.

"Nah. She's not like that. She'll love the surprise. She could never design something better than ye, Garrett, and Jane. She'd have ye do it anyway. The only difference is it will be done and here for her to enjoy."

"A bed and breakfast is an incredible idea. I can't believe I didn't think of it myself. This area is bustling with all the attention the show, *Rough Diamond*, is getting. People are flocking here to feel a part of the experience. You know that famous Kevin Costner movie quote, 'If you build, it they will come.' This is exactly what he had in mind when he said it. Darling pitstop along the way. A charming B&B in a sleepy little town with some history and character. This truly is a once in a lifetime opportunity. How soon do you think we can have it ready?"

"My goal is to unveil it right around the time the movie premieres. I hope Liv's friends will fly out and we can show all the surprises at once. Bring it all together with one big bang."

"We'll make it happen," Garrett promises.

We walk through the house so Peter and Garrett can take measurements. They are both acting like kids in a candy store. I mean, the chances of all our dreams intersecting in one giant family project; it's like winning the lottery. All of it will be designed and built with such love.

Christine and Danny, I know you both are behind this and I can't thank you enough. Our dreams continue to come true. We made it. We survived the storm.

CHAPTER THIRTEEN
(OLIVIA)

I shipped a few boxes to my mom a couple weeks ago in preparation for our three- to four-month relocation to Austin. I'll have my hands full flying by myself with Dani. This is her first flight. I hope she likes to fly. We'll soon find out. I'm armed with bottles and pacifiers in case she has trouble with her ears. I'm putting the last few items in my suitcase and we're off. We start filming in two weeks so I want to get there and get her settled into a routine beforehand. Finn wants to come on this initial trip but there is a big event scheduled at Christine's this weekend so he can't get away. We made a rule that we'll FaceTime at least twice a day so he can say good morning and good night to us, and we won't go more than fourteen days without seeing each other but we're shooting for less than ten. He'll be doing the traveling to us. We don't want to put Dani through that upheaval. It would only interrupt her schedule. Plus, Finn needs to be in Austin to oversee the building of the new restaurant. It just makes more sense. He's going to bring Frank on his first trip to stay with us at my parents while we're there. He'll be alone too much with us gone and he cannot stand being away from Dani. He adores her.

Everyone is already fighting over who gets to watch her. I'm just hoping for running water and an air mattress. I assure you no one is preparing any elaborate accommodations for me.

"My mom has an entire personal day care set up for Dani awaiting on our arrival. She keeps sending me photos. She even had my dad paint the new nursery pink so she feels more at home," I say.

"Isn't it only a two-bedroom unit?" Finn asks. He's laying with her on the bed, among the remaining piles, getting in his last few minutes of snuggle time while I finish up.

"In theory, it was supposed to be *our* guest suite when we visited. My mom was going to put a crib in it so we could all stay together. I presume I'll be in a sleeping bag next to the crib."

"I miss ye girls already. I hate this part. Saying goodbye is the worst," he says. "Dani, don't you dare get an inch bigger, do anything new, or start talking when I'm not there. Do you understand me? I won't be having it. None of it."

Jane and the twins pick us up at the airport. We drop them all off at my parents and go straight to Garrett's new store, Luxe. They officially opened eight weeks ago. The other two stores, Cotton and Gin & Tonic, back in California are running themselves at this point. He or Tristan will still need to make monthly trips back but they plan to be here for the foreseeable future. He hasn't given me too many details about this store. He's one of those people who wants the drama factor. He wants to see your face when you take it all in. We pull up to a house on the edge of a trendy neighborhood. It's a two-story, Cape Cod, cottage home. *Adorable.* What a creative concept. The house blends into the area and draws you in immediately. It's painted a soothing gray with crisp, white plantation shutters. There is an outdoor staircase adjacent to the house so you have access to both floors. He purchased the lot next door and turned it into a parking lot, which is not at all intrusive.

"Garrett gave me the top floor to use as my studio to paint my furniture," Jane says when we're pulling in.

"Ohhh, that is so great! I feel like I haven't asked you anything about this furniture line. I've been so preoccupied with everything."

"I wouldn't call almost dying while giving birth to a baby being preoccupied. I'm so glad you're here. It's been a long time since we've both been in the same place for any extended period. We'll have time to catch up now that you're here for a couple months."

"I know. I can't wait to see your new house and get familiar with the area now that you guys are all locals. Finn and I plan to find a second place here, when things settle down, since he'll have to come back and forth so frequently to monitor the new restaurant. I treasure this area. It holds such a special place in my heart. I fell in love with it when we got married here. I never thought I'd be a country type of girl, but maybe I was a cowgirl in a previous life. I love the peace and quiet; it's comforting. Add the rolling hills and toss in some water for tranquility—it's pure magic. It makes *total sense* that I live in a flat, desolate, and barren desert community," I say.

"My two favorite ladies," Garrett says.

"Wow. This is not what I was expecting but I love it," I gush, drinking it all in. The space is open and bright with soft accessories that provide a cozy, almost calming feeling. The walls are covered in shiplap and the hardwoods are painted white. The layout flows. It's broken up into multiple rooms. Each has a theme. One is Hampton beachy and another is rustic farm house. It all blends. He can make *anything* look amazing. If someone were to ask me my home decor style, the only way I could answer is to say Garrett Stanford. It would sound snobby and elitist since he's so high-end, but I can play the family card. There isn't one thing he's done that I wouldn't be proud to call my own.

"I'm evolving. It's much softer than some of the modern and industrial pieces I have at the other stores."

"I love it."

"Did Jane take you up to see her space?" he asks.

"That's where we're headed next," Jane says. We finish up the tour and go upstairs to her studio. It's one room but spacious enough for her to have storage for all the gems and treasures she collects to refurbish. She is another one with a unique talent. I don't have the eye for it. My talent came in the form of make believe.

"I never asked. What is the official name of your new painted collection?"

"The Barrington Collection."

"Ohhh, I like. Sounds very Scarlett O'Hara," I respond.

"Peter came up with it. It's the last name of a client he's working with. It sounded vintage."

"It's fitting. You're taking old things and bringing them back to life," I comment.

"That's exactly what we thought," Garrett chimes in. Jane has a little sitting area with two fluffy white chairs and a love seat in the back part of the room for her breaks, so we take a load off.

"I'll be using two of her pieces in the upcoming *Rough Diamond* episode," He says.

"When do you start shooting?" I ask.

"We're almost done. We're taking some final shots this week then it will go to editing."

"I had no idea. That's so exciting. I can't wait to see it. We're both going to be movie stars. Well, a real movie star will be portraying me on camera . . . but similar," I say.

"How are you feeling about all of the excitement coming up for you?" Jane asks.

"I've not had much time to think about it. I mean, it's not like I have a role or am responsible for anything. I just show up. It's so kind of Mac to include me. He wants to ensure I have creative input so it translates on screen. They're renting a house during filming, too. Jules said she'll come to set to keep me company a few days a week. I have no idea what I'm doing, but it will be fun to be part of the process. Mac said he would have the full shooting schedule to me by early next week. I want to enjoy the next couple weeks hanging out with you guys, and Mom and Dad. Take advantage of all of my babysitters."

"How is Jules' brother, Kevin, doing?" Jane asks.

"Ugh. It's so sad. His ALS is worsening more and more every day. I don't think he'll make it through summer."

"That is so, so sad. The worst part of it is they're the best of friends, aren't they? I can't imagine losing one of you guys. It's heartbreaking to think about. He's so young," Jane says.

"She'll be traveling back a bunch to see him and help out where she can," I say.

"Let us know if there is anything we can do. Donations seems like a cop out. Anyone can give money but what do they need?" Garrett asks.

"They need love, support, and prayers," I say.

Day one of shooting is here. It's surreal that my story, *The Man Guide*, is being made into a movie. It's a romantic comedy about a character, Claire Stevens, loosely based on my life. She has a guardian angel, think *Bruce* or *Evan Almighty*, appear, giving her advice on love and life. She ignores him because she doesn't subscribe to the idea that she could, in any way, communicate with the beyond. She thinks his presence is a series of coincidences. She's bound and determined to control her own destiny. Each time she ignores his advice, her life hits another dead-end and he reappears to remind her she's on the wrong path. When she finally gives in and listens, her life takes a dramatic turn and everything falls into place.

Mac told me to plan for long days. Filming can last anywhere from ten to fourteen hours. Call time for the actors is five thirty. I have a baby and five thirty is even pushing it for *me*. I can't imagine these hot, young actors are any more thrilled about it. My instinct is to swing by and pick up a couple carafes of coffee and dozens of donuts to allow the caffeine and sugar to fuel the day but people in Hollywood don't eat fattening food. Then I remember hearing about the craft services catering to these A-listers, so I order myself a giant latte and am on my way. Shooting is in McKinney Falls State Park today. The scene about the main character, Claire, who is out on an early morning solo hike when she slips, falls, and breaks her foot. *Cue the hero*. The funny, handsome, single guy named Connor happens upon her while hiking with his dog, Hank. This is their meet cute.

Danny, is this truly happening? Are they really making a movie based on my life? I can't even remember how I got here. It's such a blur. All I know is I moved, inch by inch, with periods of long pauses, then finally crossed over the threshold into a whole new, mesmerizing world. This is surreal. Beyond my wildest dreams. Bigger and brighter than I could've ever imagined. It's only now, looking back, I realize how far I've come. The pain I've experienced forced an enormous amount of strength to settle in. Like a seed being planted that needed constant care and nurturing is now blossoming. Each passing day, I've doubted my will, my tenacity, my resolve and ability to go on, and now I'm here because you carried me every step of the way. Your friendship is overwhelming and for that I'm eternally grateful.

As I pull into the parking lot, I see the equipment trucks and a crowd of people. I'm going in blind and have no idea what to expect. *Here goes nothing.*

As movie watchers, we take for granted the energy that is not only put into one scene, but the entire final movie production. It takes a few days for me to grasp the enormity of the process. The number of resources include staff for multiple cameras, props, lighting, wardrobe, makeup, dining, and production. This is all in addition to the actors, crew, and directors. At the end of every day, a progress report is shared to outline budget spending in all areas of the film, including extras. Being in the corporate world for such a long time, it's like project management on a very large project. Lots of moving parts, tons of coordination, and all bound by time. Staying on schedule is crucial, but there are many variables that can interfere with shooting. For example, outdoor locations can be impacted by weather along with other factors. It can get dicey so flexibility is the key.

Jane brought Dani down to set a couple times this week to visit. Mac arranged for Jules and me to have a trailer where we can rest in between takes. We're on our way back there now to eat some lunch. Being together so much has worked out well for both of us. It's hard being away from Finn for weeks at a time, and Jules needs the distraction with Mac being so preoccupied.

"Did I tell you I spoke to my sister-in-law? She mentioned Kevin's been writing letters to the kids for all their major life milestones like their graduations and weddings," she says.

"Oh my God," I lament.

"She's also asked us and several of his close friends to write letters, telling him how special he is and how much he means to us and everyone he encounters. She thinks it will really cheer him up and then they will have the letters to read and cherish when he's gone."

"It's wonderful, beautiful, and so gut-wrenchingly unimaginable," I respond. "I've experienced loss. It's all gut-wrenching, but Dan was ripped away. I didn't have to witness his deterioration. It's unthinkable to feel so helpless, unable to help your own brother," I say.

"There are no words. It's indescribable. I feel like all I do is cry. I try to be strong for all of them but we're all grieving. Of course, we want an end to his pain and suffering. We want him to be at peace, but how am I ever going to say goodbye?" she says, dissolving into tears. I hug her. It's overwhelming to grasp the magnitude of this horrific illness. I want to do whatever I can to support Jules. She is a remarkable woman. I am in awe of her unwavering strength. It's all beyond comprehension. I keep asking Danny and Christine to welcome Kevin with open arms and to save him a spot at the bar. What an incredible team they're building up there. Each one has a special purpose and we need each one of them to hold us up.

CHAPTER FOURTEEN
(FINN)

We're always closed on Mondays, but tonight is the dedication ceremony for Christie at Christine's. I think Tex might be more excited about this than proposing. Liv still has no idea. It hasn't been hard keeping any of this from her because she's so distracted with filming in Austin. I never keep anything from her but this will make my plan even more special. The timing couldn't be better.

I'm taking the lead on all the preparations. I have a couple surprises up my sleeve for Tex, too. I want this to be special for him. Christie thinks we're having a restaurant anniversary party for all the staff. I've been running around all morning, arranging the last-minute details. Preparations are in full swing in the kitchen.

"Alrighty, laddie, this is your cue to leave," I say, taking the knife out of Tex's hand and escorting him to the door.

"Whaddya mean? I reckon we got way more to do," he says, confused.

"Quit yer bellyachin'. I reckon I got more to do. You get home and spend time with your lassie. I'm having a car pick ye up at seven. I don't want to see ye back here until then."

"What are ya fixin' to do?" he asks.

"Ye'll see tonight. Now get out of here."

I gather the team and reveal the plan. We'll be serving a family style, Italian themed meal tonight. It'll be infused with some of Christie's renowned family recipes: individual chicken parmesan bites; mushroom farfalle pasta with goat cheese; Grandma's white chicken and cheese lasagna recipe; a bruschetta bar; and spicy individual pizzas with truffle oil, arugula, green onion, asparagus, olives, fresh spinach, and buffalo mozzarella. Dessert will be cannoli and tiramisu, and we're making a specialty cocktail called "The Christie." It's a white chocolate and Kahlua martini surprise.

A red carpet for the restaurant entrance where they'll have their photo taken upon their arrival. I've also invited other local media outlets. The staff put together a slide collage with photos from their engagement and wedding.

#

They arrive and Christie still has no idea this evening is set up for her. She thinks the limo and media attention are for Tex because he's an owner. It isn't until her family starts to arrive that she becomes suspicious. Let the ceremony *begin*.

"Good evening, everyone. Thank ye all for coming. Tonight is a special evening within the history of Christine's. Tex's and my partnership started several years ago in the dazzling city of New York and ended up here, thousands of miles away, surrounded by palm trees in the middle of the desert. Our journeys paved a similar path. We've both seen our fair share of rainy days and rough terrain, but we ended up here in the sun. Palm Springs has been generous to us. It's allowed us to pursue our culinary dreams. We've both poured our blood, sweat, and tears into this restaurant. During that time, we've each personally transformed. We both met our better halfs here. The lassies that make our worlds go-round. That's why we are all here tonight. It's time for a new chapter, for growth and expansion. Tex and I are opening a new restaurant in Austin, Texas. We both know the amount of time and dedication one restaurant takes, much less two and in different states. We've decided that while this partnership remains strong, it's time to divide and conquer. Liv's family has recently relocated to Austin, so she and I will make Texas our home base. I'll take over the day to day tasks and management of the new place. Tex will stay here and be taking the reins of Christine's full time. Lucky for us, his wife's name happens to be Christine. I'd like to welcome our town Mayor, Bill Dodson, who will be performing a ribbon-cutting ceremony to dedicate Christine's, and transfer the title, to Mrs. Christine Bolt. Here is your new golden key," I say when everyone erupts into cheers and applause. Christie is visibly stunned and overwhelmed. She can't stop hugging and kissing Tex. We dim the lights and the slide show starts. The cherry on top of this fabulous moment. A few minutes later, when things die down, Tex takes the mic.

"Good evening, y'all. Thanks for coming. Christie and I couldn't imagine enjoying this moment without any of ya. I reckon y'all have been here for every step of this crazy trek. We're grateful. Thanks for always bein' so supportive of all of us . . . and Scottie, I've got a bit of a surprise of my own." I'm confused. This night is all about them. I have no idea what he could possibly have for me.

"Team, please help do me the honors," Tex says as they approach me and hand me a small, rectangular box with a ribbon on it. It looks like a jewelry box big enough for a bracelet. I'm perplexed. I open it to uncover a sterling silver spoon. I take it out of the box and hold it up to investigate further.

"Are ye trying to tell me Dani will be growing up a spoiled princess?" I ask.

"Nah, I reckon you're keen on signs and symbols. This is my symbol for telling ya we just earned our first Michelin star," he says.

"*Whaaaat? Yer lying. How? When?*" I ask in amazement.

"I found out last week. Ya were in Austin when I got the call. I knew we'd all be together tonight, so I thought I'd give ya a surprise send-off as well."

"This is brilliant. Glorious. Bloody *fantastic.* Champagne for everyone," I call out.

"I reckon ya got a wife to talk to. Go call Liv and share the news," he says and we share a bro hug.

"This is smashing," I whisper and duck into the office to FaceTime Liv to share the news. We both cry. This time they're happy tears. Our dreams are finally coming true. I miss my girls. I can't wait to see them.

We don't have much time to celebrate. Liv calls me first thing in the morning to inform me that Jules' brother Kevin died. Jules flew back last weekend and was with him when he passed. He was surrounded by family and went peacefully. We're both devastated for all of them. Liv is flying home tomorrow so we can attend the services.

The homily at Mass is the most beautiful and poignant I've heard. Kevin was active in his parish before his diagnosis, so he knew the members of the church and clergy well. They all came together as a community to support him. They helped prepare his home at each progressive stage. They were instrumental in raising money, at both of our fundraisers, to help offset costs and replenish savings for his kid's colleges funds. The priest who said Mass was involved with Kevin and the family for many months before his passing. They had several frank conversations about preparing for the end of life. His sermon was personal.

"Brothers and sisters, we gather here today to celebrate the life of our brother, Kevin. He was welcomed into the kingdom of heaven and joins our savior, Jesus Christ. I've known Kevin for some time. He was a kind and generous soul. He was selfless, humble, and charismatic. His love of music was only surpassed by the tremendous amount of love he had for his family and friends. This disease has taken its toll on everyone around him, especially his wife, children, and sister who had a special closeness to him. I've been working on this homily for months since we had the conversation about his wishes. He asked about the Anointing of the Sick, Last Rites, and the Church's position on cremation. He wanted to know about the afterlife and my personal beliefs. Conversations many of us are not prepared for, including his children, who were forced to grow up much sooner than their time. He tackled the conversations head on with strength and bravery. He had faith he was going to a better place where he'd be free of pain, where he could live again. It's only those of us who are left behind who struggle with our faith. The only way to explain, in terms that may be relatable, is to talk about an unborn baby in their mother's womb. Imagine your job is to convince the unborn baby that outside of their safe and isolating cocoon, a vast world exists. A vibrant universe full of love and hope. A place they could never imagine. All they know is this warm, safe place with a lifeline connected to their mother. How successful do you think you would be? Do you think they would understand what you meant by the sun is ablaze and beaming with warmth, allowing brilliant flowers to grow, or the night sky has stars that shine so bright it lights up a planet? No, they must experience it to believe it in all its glory. There isn't any way to adequately describe it. The same amount of faith and trust is required for your transition into the afterlife. No one can describe it, because we won't experience it until we get there. My faith is strong. I believe, and have hope, knowing I can't comprehend the enormity of what lies ahead. Seek comfort in your faith. Faith is belief in what you cannot see."

Liv and I are on the same flight as Jules and Mac. We're all flying back to Austin. This is when everything gets real. When all your family and friends go back to their lives and you are left alone with the darkness. Mac and Jules, quite literally, saved my life when I lost Christine. We need to embrace them so they feel loved and supported.

Christine, it's so hard to be joyful when the people around us are experiencing such sadness. Liv and I have all these great things going on, and now Jules and Mac are devastated. Jules is broken. We all know this sadness. How hard it is. How it never goes away. It starts to briefly fade then it comes back like a tsunami wave and drowns you all over again. It's like giant chunks of your heart are ripped off. We eventually mend parts of them back together but the scars and gaps are deep. Please help all of them. Give them strength. They need hope.

We see them sitting at the gate when we arrive.

"Hi guys," Liv says.

"Hey," Jules replies.

"How did everything go last night after we left?" I ask.

"Everyone left by nine. We were exhausted," she says. "Just to add to it, I ended up throwing up all night."

"Oh no, do you think you got food poisoning?" Liv asks.

"That's what we thought, but Mac felt fine. Then I started realizing that for the last couple weeks I've felt waves of nausea. I assumed it was the stress with everything going on until the pregnancy test I took this morning proved that theory wrong," Jules says.

"Ohhhhh, this is such wonderful news. Timing is bittersweet but it's almost as if Kevin left you this precious gift of life on his way back home," Liv says, hugging Jules, and they both break down in tears.

Prayers answered. Thank ye, Christine.

Filming is on schedule so Liv is back to her routine. I'm meeting Garrett and Peter out at the Barrington property today. I guess it's now the McDaniels estate. We paid cash so we closed within fifteen days. The family was anxious to close the transaction. The B&B and the restaurant renovations are well underway. The remaining permits are in place for breaking ground on the new house. Peter has the crew lined up and we're going over the final plans to make any last-minute tweaks. It's important to get this one right. This is our dream home and we'll be establishing roots for years and generations to come. This is where Dani will grow up and likely where Liv and I will retire.

We do a walkthrough of both buildings then drive out to the area where the house will stand. I'm building a six-bedroom, six-thousand-square-foot farm house. We don't need that much space but we will want to host groups of friends for extended periods of time. Liv is such a social person. Her friends mean everything to her. It's important for me to create an environment that encourages people to visit. We have the means to do it and this will ensure they are comfortable and can spread out. I can see it now. We'll label the rooms: the Liza, Alexa, and Red Suites.

I'm having a two-thousand-square-foot guest house built as well for my parents who will be visiting from Scotland. The casita will be one level so, as they age, they won't have to worry about navigating stairs. It will give them peace, quiet, and privacy when they want it. My goal is to build a family compound that is both inviting and welcoming.

The house will back up to the biggest of the three lakes on the property. It will have a large infinity pool with a hot tub, outdoor kitchen, a large area for a fire pit, and surrounded by Adirondack chairs, creating an outdoor oasis. The back of the house will be covered in a wall of windows, facing west so we can see the sunset. The first floor will be an open concept with a large, oversized living room, so everyone can gather in one place. The chef-grade kitchen will be massive as well.

We'll have two separate bedroom suites, on the first floor, on opposite sides of the house. The remaining four bedrooms will be upstairs. The room I am most excited about is the large studio I'm building for Liv where she can write her future novels and screenplays. I'm concerned about the bones and layout. I'll leave it to Garrett to decorate. It's going to be the best surprise *ever*.

CHAPTER FIFTEEN
(OLIVIA)

This Saturday is Dani's first birthday. We're having a party for her at my parents' house, then I'm surprising Finn with an overnight as a celebration for winning his Michelin star. We've both been so busy we haven't had much us time. I want to do something sexy for him.

We're up early putting on the final touches for the party. Finn is barbecuing for everyone. I run to pick up the balloons and the cake. The party is angel themed. Dani is our sweet little angel and we know she is being watched over and protected by our special guardian angels, Danny and Christine, so it's a no-brainer. We're not going overboard on decorations: just pastel balloons, streamers, and a couple birthday signs. We're keeping it simple. I made a couple goodie bags for the twins.

We set up a scholarship in Kevin's name that we plan to contribute to for each major milestone or event. Dani has plenty. We don't need her being even more spoiled. We want her to grow up understanding the value of hard work and know what it means to be charitable. We will continue to volunteer with her, especially for ALS, so she knows how important it is to help those who are less fortunate.

Jules, Mac, Garrett, and Tristan are the only guests coming in addition to Jane's family.

"Happy birthday, sweetie," Garrett says as he enters with arms full of gift bags and presents. Tristan is in tow with cookies, cupcakes, and a piñata. They can see the look of disapproval on my face. "Before you get all judgey on me, here is a check for five thousand dollars for the scholarship in Kevin's name. Now can I give her a tutu or two without being hassled?" he finishes.

"I'll allow it only because she's too young to understand how over the top Uncle GG is," I reply, relieving them of some of their load.

We spend a couple hours chatting and enjoying the feast Finn made, and cut the cake before Dani goes down for her nap. We got her a smash cake for her to dive into, but, first, we set the big cake in front of her for the photo op. It's a three-tiered vanilla cake with pink buttercream frosting and angel dust sprinkled on it. We keep it far enough away so she can't reach the lit candle while we sing happy birthday to her. She is hesitant, looking around to determine why we're all staring at her, smiling and singing the same words. Once we start clapping, she joins in, and we place the small cake in front of her. She's not sure what to do with it so Finn runs his finger over the icing and puts it in her mouth to taste.

"Yummy," he says and her face lights up as soon as it crosses her lips. No further encouragement needed. She dives in, grabbing handfuls. We had to take it away. Garrett opened her presents for her. A few books, several darling outfits, and three tutus, because a girl can't ever have *too many*.

"I love how she plays with your charm bracelet when you reach over her," Garrett observes.

"Yes, anytime I feed her she plays with it. She always has it in her hand. It's sweet since they all have such special meaning. It's like she is connected to it," I reply.

"What does she want now?" Dani keeps pointing and saying 'baba.' I refill her sippy cup with milk, hand it back to her, and she pushes it away and cries.

"She's been doing this a lot lately. We think she's asking for more milk or a bottle but each time we give it to her, she refuses it then points and gestures for more in sign language. She's not saying 'dada.' She knows Finn is dada and always uses it in the right context. We can't figure it out."

"What's with this bear that looks like it's been around since the early nineteen hundreds?" he asks.

"It's Dan's bear from when he was little. His mom had Red bring it out to me. It's become one of Dani's favorite things. She won't let it out of her sight. Her three favorite things? Her stuffy, my charm bracelet, and Frank, her fluffy."

"Aw, that's cute. I'll let you play with a mangled teddy bear sweetie since it has so much history," he says to Dani.

Finn and I put Dani down for a nap after everyone leaves.

"Now it's time for your surprise," I say to Finn.

"Aye, that sounds enticing." He grabs me by the waist and pulls me in close for a kiss. "Aren't your mum and da going to wonder where we are?" he asks, continuing to nibble my ear.

"Hold your horses for a minute, laddie. We'll have more privacy soon," I say, kissing him.

"Aye?"

"Yes, pack a change of clothes. We'll be gone overnight. We haven't had time to celebrate your Michelin star so it's time I make it up to you."

"Mm, but what if I can't wait that long?" he asks, grabbing my ass.

"It's all part of the anticipation," I tease.

I blindfold him before we leave my parents' house so he doesn't know the route we're taking.

"Ye can pull right back into the garage for all I care. The blindfold is gift enough. Go ahead and take advantage of me right here, I won't resist," he says.

"It won't be long. Hang tight."

We're in the car just under thirty minutes when we pull into the parking lot. I get out to go check-in then come back to Finn's side of the car and open his door, helping him out. I position him at the perfect angle and unveil the surprise. I had Garrett drop off a couple bags and a cooler earlier this morning. I packed a picnic with cheese, crackers, prosciutto, grapes, strawberries, and a couple bottles of champagne.

"*Bloody fantastic.* It's our honeymoon suite. Yer amazing. How thoughtful. Thank ye, love," he says, kissing me. I put his face in my hands and lean in to look deep in his eyes.

"You're welcome. I want you to always know how much I love you. I'm unbelievably proud of you. A Michelin star is an *amazing* honor. You're now part of an elite club. You deserve every bit of this attention. I'm blown away by your talent. You make it look effortless. Your passion inspires me. I don't want to ever take who you are or what we have for granted. You're the light of my life and now I want to show you how much you mean to me."

He picks me up and carries me over the threshold and has my clothes off before we hit the bed. We make love all afternoon.

He draws a bubble bath while I pour us some bubbly. We climb in to relax and enjoy the moment.

"I miss this . . . Us," he says, caressing my hair and shoulders.

"Me, too. We have so many incredible things going on, so much to be grateful for but I long for the days where you, Dani, and I can be settled, permanently, in one place and call it home. With the new restaurant, you'll be traveling back and forth but I hope you and Tex can work out a schedule where you'll have long periods with us. I can't believe we celebrated Dani's first birthday today. Time is flying. Before you know it, she'll be walking and talking. Is Palm Springs the place we want to raise her? My family is all here now. Maybe we should consider a move here?"

"I think we can buy something here. A townhome or small house. Something low maintenance so there won't be any upkeep. You and Dani can stay for stretches of time. You can write from anywhere."

"I know but what happens when she starts school? She won't be able to be away. She'll make friends. We won't want to uproot her."

"That's still five years from now; we have plenty of time to worry about that. So much can change in five years. I mean, we haven't even known each other for five years. In less than that time, think about everything that's occurred. We met, moved, got married, had a baby, yer filming a movie, and we're opening a new restaurant."

"I guess when you put it that way, it makes more sense. I just don't want to lose sight of it. My parents are getting older. It would be nice for us to all be together."

"We'll sort it out. Don't fret love. Right in this exact moment, I have more feasting to do . . . on ye."

#

In the middle of the night, I'm startled awake up, gasping for air, and sit up in bed. I scare Finn.

"Love, what is it? Are ye okay?"

"Oh my gosh. I had the most vivid dream . . . *of Dan*," I say through tears.

"What was it about?" he asks, comforting me.

"I've never experienced anything like it. I'm certain it was a real encounter with him," I continue. "I got a call from his parents saying they had a surprise for me and I needed to come over. When I got there, they revealed that Dan came back from heaven, for one day, and he wanted to see me because he had a message for me. I, of course, was in shock and disbelief but I rushed up to his bedroom and there he was sitting on his bed —just like I remember. He looked perfect. Those baby blue eyes and dimples for days. He was wearing his favorite blue jeans, a plaid button-down shirt, and his Chucks." I start to sob. "I couldn't believe it. I was blubbering and wouldn't let go. I kept hugging him while he comforted me. He sat me down and said, 'Hank, God will only allow me this one visitation so you need to listen to me carefully. I see and hear everything. I am *always* with you, no matter what. You need to continue to trust me, to believe and have faith. You're special. God's given you a special gift. He knows you're listening and can interpret all the signs and symbols I'm sending. You've been chosen to help others, to connect them, through the belief in signs and symbols, with their loved ones on the other side, to give them hope. This movie is going to bring attention and shed light on the afterlife in a practical and relatable way. You're making sense of the communication channel between our two worlds. It will resonate and bring comfort to countless others who are desperate to be in touch. Your job is to teach them, to arm them with the tools to understand how to listen and decode their loved one's messages. We are all safe. You don't need to overthink. It's us when you hear a special song or see a butterfly, bird, rainbow, or a license plate. We convey our presence in subtle ways. They are not coincidences. Believe. You are on the path to your destiny. Stop doubting and know, more than anything, that I will love you and miss you forever.' And then he was gone. I couldn't ask him anything. I had so many questions and he was just gone. That's when I woke up," I lament.

"Oh love, I'm so sorry," Finn says, holding me.

"It was him, Finn. It was 100 percent Danny. I have zero doubt. None."

He doesn't say anything else; he just holds and consoles me until I drift back off to sleep.

CHAPTER SIXTEEN
(FINN)

Mac and Jules are back in Austin for final scene takes for the film. The movie is in the last stages of post-production editing then the marketing blitz will begin. The movie is scheduled to come out late fall, just before Thanksgiving. Mac and I are hitting the town tonight. I'm bringing him in on my grand plan so everything goes off without a hitch. We have a drink with the girls at their hotel then we're off for a guys' night. The first stop is the new B&B and restaurant. Both of us have been so busy, I haven't had time to share the news. I fill him in on all the details on the ride out. He cannot contain his excitement as we pull up to walk the property. The B&B and restaurant are done. Garrett has been moving all the furnishings. He is just waiting on the final accessories. He's now focused on our house, which should be ready in the next six weeks. It lines up perfectly with the movie premiere.

"Laddie, this is bloody brilliant. Absolutely glorious," he says as we climb the steps to the porch of the B&B. The overall theme is a combination of rustic cowboy and shabby chic. It's a blend of textures. The wrap-around, covered front porch, is lined with white rocking chairs. You enter into a great room with a floor to ceiling cobblestone fireplace adorned with a large set of longhorns. Oversized leather couches, chairs, and ottomans cover a patterned, faux calf hair area rug overlooking the patio. The wall of glass doors brings the outside in. They open onto a sprawling brick patio with a dozen Adirondack chairs surrounding a fire pit. A hot tub overlooks the sprawling property and rolling hills in the distance. The kitchen and dining room fill up the remainder of the first floor where guests will be served a fresh farm-to-table breakfast every morning.

We continue the tour upstairs to the eight bedrooms. We did some reconfiguration so each room could have its own private bathroom. Each suite is donned with a plaque named in honor of each of our loved ones: McDaniels, Henry, Stanford, Hill, Bolt, Sullivan, Frances, and The Barrington to preserve the history of the estate. Each is decorated based on the family background or location. The McDaniels is decorated like an old Irish cottage, and the Henry is a Roaring Twenties, Chicago-style gangster theme. It's been such a fun and exciting project, and it's turned out even more brilliant than I dreamed.

"This is your suite," I say as we enter. The back wall has a floor to ceiling mural of the New York City skyline and Brooklyn Bridge. The room is monochromatic. It has a soft gray wallpaper lining the walls with grand window panels covering the windows. Two French provincial chairs bookend the old fireplace with sconces and a lofty mirror above the mantle. The king-size bed has crisp white bedding with a modern chandelier hanging above it.

"It's smashing. Bloody fantastic. Better than any five-star hotel I've been to. Each room has a different tone but it comes together brilliantly," Mac says.

"It's all Garrett. His taste is exquisite. You give him any canvas and he nails it," I reply. "Tex's room is one of the best," I say as we visit there next. The walls are covered in old, restored barn wood. It has a metal bedframe with a dozen cowboy hats hanging above the headboard. An old antique gun rests above the bathroom door and the variety of accessories include a wagon wheel floor lamp.

"Where does he find this stuff?" Mac asks, picking up the spurred cowboy boots resting on the fireplace hearth.

"I have no idea. I don't ask. I just write checks."

Next stop is the barn that's been converted into the new restaurant. The grounds are expansive. They host dozens of picnic tables to let guests enjoy the environment while they wait. We'll hire live bands for entertainment. There will be a small retail store where they can shop and buy merchandise, like hats and t-shirts. Tex plans to bottle his own brand of BBQ sauce.

The outside of the restaurant still looks like a barn, as we tried to preserve as much of the character as we could to add to the ambience. Inside, Garrett replicated our wedding reception concept. Upscale casual. Long, wooden, picnic-table-style dining with white linen table cloths and a mixture of painted chairs. Fabric hangs from the rafters and chandeliers dangle from the ceiling while white lights wrap around pillars throughout the space.

"Glorious. Liv will be speechless," he says.

"Beyond my wildest dreams, "I admit.

We make one last stop at the house and then drive back into town. We go to a local joint, known for its bourbon, and belly up to the bar. The bartender serves us our first round.

"I'd like to make a toast. To my brother and best, lifelong lad who's been with me through thick and thin, every single step of the way," I say, raising my glass.

"Cheers to that. Did ye ever imagine we'd make it out of our small town much less make something of ourselves? Ye have a Michelin star for Christ's sake," he jokes.

"And ye are a highly sought-after comedy writer. We swindled them —all of them," I add. "How the hell did we get so blessed?"

"I don't know but let's not jinx it," he says. "It hasn't always been rainbows but we've had each other's back along the way and for that I am truly grateful."

"How's Jules doing?" I ask.

"It's tough as ye'd expect. She's trying to concentrate on preparing for the baby when she's not traveling with me. She's taken on more volunteering with the ALS Foundation, trying to keep herself busy and distracted but it's going to be a long road."

"The baby arriving will help. It will not only fill her time but the love and joy this baby will bring is indescribable. I never knew I could love anything so much. Are you guys going to find out what you're having?" I ask.

"No, we want to build up to the surprise. It's adding another level to the excitement."

"Well, I need your help to deliver this surprise."

"I can't believe Liv has no clue," he says.

"She's been so wrapped up with filming, Dani, and visiting with her family that she's let me handle the restaurant. She's going to be blown away. I can't wait. We were just away and she was saying how she wants to feel rooted and settled in one place. I brushed her off, saying we have time to plan long term for Dani's schooling. She has no idea. You, Dick, Peter, and

Garrett are my cavalry on this one so no sharing with Jules. We're so close I can't afford to have it leaked at this stage."

"Not a word. How are you going to unveil it?" he asks.

"That's where I'm hoping you come in. I presume you are planning on a premiere?"

"Aye," he confirms.

I've learned so much from Mac with him being in the industry. There is almost a science behind choosing a release date. Certain movies perform better at specific times during the year. This is a light-hearted, romantic, feel good movie so will be perfect for the holidays.

"We're hosting the press junket here in Austin to build hype since the movie was shot here," he adds. Junkets include media journalists, entertainment reporters, and movie critics. They are flown out to a special day of interviews with the actors and creators of the film. Weeks before the movie opens nationwide, the promotions start. The idea is to bombard the public with so many images for the movie that it becomes a ""can't miss" event. The actors will start working the major talk show circuit; billboards and busses will be covered in gigantic ads. Marketers will run tons of teaser trailers on TV and place full-page ads in major newspapers and magazines.

"We'll have a small premiere here in Austin for the locals as a thank you for hosting us in this amazing city," he adds.

"Is it normally a private, invitation-only event?" I ask.

"It depends, why?"

"I would love to have Liv's friends and family there to surprise her. We can plan the event the night before

I have a pre-Grand Opening at the restaurant. We can tell her you asked me to host the cast party at the new place so we can get publicity. I would stage that as the unveiling and she'll have everyone she loves there to witness it," I suggest.

"Brilliant. Yes, let's do it."

"My only other question is where do you plan to have the premiere? Do you have a theater picked out? Does it have to host a certain amount of people?"

"Nothing is locked in so we have options. Why? What are you thinking?"

"Well, Liv has this fun memory with Danny. They went to see *Wedding Crashers* at an old theater near her hometown, called the Tivoli. They got busted smuggling beer in and got kicked out. I did some research and there is an old theater here in Austin called the Ritz, which has the exact same vibe. I thought it would be special to host it there so she'd almost feel like Danny is there with her."

"How many does it hold?" he asks.

"One hundred and seventy-five."

"If you can keep her invite list to thirty or under, that would be perfect. That will still be plenty of room for the cast, crew, and local contributors. Consider it done."

"Fantastic. I'll get to work," I say.

"I've actually got a surprise for ye," he says.

"Aye?"

"Jules and I are also here to look at buying another home. Once the baby arrives, I plan to take more time off between projects so we can slow down a bit. Jules feels so connected to Austin after spending so much time here. Plus, she wants the baby to grow up near her cousin Dani."

"That's the best news I've heard all year. Welcome, brother," I say, as we signal the bartender for another round.

I made all the arrangements to get Red, Liza, and Alexa here for the movie premiere. Everyone is onboard only knowing the first part of the surprise. Liv has no idea. She thinks she and I get to attend the premiere as Mac and Jules' guests. The plan is to have everyone waiting inside after she walks the red carpet.

Today is the day. I ship Liv off to get her hair and makeup done while I run out to the restaurant to take care of all the final details. There is only a couple hour gap between the premiere and the cast arrival for dinner. I needed to space it out enough so she and I can have some alone time while I reveal our future. We'll be sleeping in our new house tonight. I can barely contain my excitement.

I meet her at the hotel where she is getting ready with Jules. I knock on the door and she opens it and takes my breath away. She's standing there in a spaghetti strap, pale pink, full-length gown with a sweetheart neckline, sequins covering the bodice. The fabric clings to her body. Her hair is pulled up and back off her face and her makeup is soft but stunning.

"Ye look smashing."

"Aw, thanks love. You don't look so bad yourself," she says, as she drinks me in, standing there in my tuxedo. "I must say we do clean up well."

"The limo is downstairs; are you ready to go?" I ask.

"Yes, Mac and Jules left a half hour ago. They had to get there early to do some press interviews."

When we get to the limo, I have celebratory champagne waiting for us.

"Has it sunk in yet that we're driving over to *yer* movie premiere?" I ask.

"Pinch me just in case," she jokes.

"I'd like to make a toast to my stunning, talented, and entertaining wife whom I love beyond measure. I know what it took ye to get here to this moment. Yer resilience, tenacity, and resolve is nothing short of astonishing. Ye inspire me every single day. Dani is blessed to have such a strong, generous, and confident mum to look up to. I'm so proud of ye, Liv. Cheers to ye." I raise my glass.

"Cheers, my love. Right back at you. We're turning into quite the little power couple," she quips.

The limo pulls up and she sees the theater.

"Aw. The theater reminds me of the place back home I went to with Danny when we got kicked out." The surprise is off to a glorious start. We stand in line to get our picture taken in front of the sponsor screen. We're up next and they take several photos of just Liv then a handful of us together and we make our way inside. I had everyone stand in a certain area, just out of sight, so she'd see everyone all at once. I catch Red out of the corner of my eye and start to escort Liv over when she stops dead in her tracks. She sees everyone in the crowd and begins to cry.

"Did you do this?" she says.

"Aye. Surprise," I whisper.

"Finn McDaniels, *thank you*. I love you so much," she says as Red, Alexa, and Liza smother her in hugs and kisses. She's thrilled to have them here to celebrate this monumental night. Mac arranged for all of us to sit together in one section. Just before we sit down, I see Red hand Liv something and they exchange words. I'm not close enough to hear their conversation but Liv broke down in tears, so whatever it was, was special.

I'm trying not to be biased but I'd say we have a winner on our hands. Everyone laughed and cried. It was a sweet storyline of faith and hope. Mac did a phenomenal job of capturing the essence of the story. Liv is happy, which is the most important thing. Mac announces that the party will be moving over to the new restaurant and passes out address details.

Liv and I get in the limo.

"I saw Red hand ye something just before the movie started. Ye got emotional. What was it?" I ask.

"She was cleaning out boxes from her parents' basement and came across my yearbook. I gave it to her to sign the last summer after graduation and we both forgot about it. Her mom must have packed it away thinking it was hers, but it was mine. Red found it and thought this was the perfect opportunity to give it to me. Dan had signed it," she shares.

"What does it say?"

She opens the yearbook, takes a deep breath, trying to hold back her tears, and reads it to me.

My beloved Hank,

Where do I start? Here we are at the end of the road with endless possibilities ahead. I wish I could say I was nothing but excited but if I'm being honest, I'm more apprehensive and anxious. The unknown can be a scary place, especially when you know what you're leaving behind. I can say, without a doubt, that these last four years in high school were the best of my life.

The reason for that is largely due to you and our forever friendship. I know we're going to be physically separated now but you will always be in my heart. Nothing can ever break our unique and special bond. You are one of a kind and I'll never be lucky enough to meet another girl like you. Although we never had a romantic connection, I do believe you are one of my soulmates and we'll always be deeply connected. We don't need to see each other to understand how special this is. We will know in our souls. I wish you the best on the amazing journey ahead. No matter where I am, I will always be your biggest cheerleader. Now go kick some ass!

I love you forever,

Daniel

I reach over to console her as she sobs.

"I never read it before today. It's almost as if it was meant for me to see in this exact moment. How does he do that? He blows me away."

"I know. There isn't any explaining it," I say as the limo pulls up in front of Liv's parents' house.

"Where are we? I thought we were going to the restaurant," she says, looking around, confused.

"I want both my girls to see the restaurant together for the first time. We can't take a tour without our sweet Dani, so we're here to bring her along. I'll install the car seat while you go get her."

CHAPTER SEVENTEEN
(OLIVIA)

"What a terrific idea to have the cast dinner at the new restaurant. It will give us exposure and now my girls are here to see it, too," I say.

"It seemed to align perfectly. I told the local media to come out and we can both get coverage," Finn replies.

"I can't wait to see it. Do you think I abandoned you during this process? I feel like I've been MIA this entire time with filming and taking care of Dani. I'm not going to lie; I'm excited I'm going in blind. I don't have any expectation so it will make seeing it that much more special. I have no doubt it will be fabulous."

"Speaking of going in blind, it's my turn to blindfold you, now put this on," he says as he hands me the blindfold. I agree with him. The blindfold adds another layer of excitement. We'll have to introduce this in the bedroom, *stat*.

"Okay, we're here. We're going to see it in stages so keep your blindfold on. I'll hold Dani and lead the way," he says, helping me out of the car. We walk about a hundred yards and stop. He prompts me to take off my blindfold and in front of me stands a beautiful old home.

"Oh wow, this is beautiful. This isn't what I was envisioning but this is fabulous," I say.

"Liv, this isn't the restaurant. This is our new B&B."

I get through my shock and awe, and he explains the history behind the property.

"It's gorgeous but how are we going to run a B&B from California?" I ask.

"It's going to be a family business. Your parents, Jane, Peter, Garrett, and Tristan have all agreed to help run this place. We wanted to have a legacy in the family, something to leave for Dani and the twins someday," he says and begins to take me on a tour. With each step, I'm falling more and more in love. I see each of the name plates and tears start to fall.

"This is amazing, Finn. How on earth did you keep this from me all this time? I can't believe the amount of work that had to go into this place. Dani, do you like it?" I ask, spinning her around in the hallway.

"This has been Peter and Garrett's pet project for the better part of the last year," he says.

"Wait, does Jane know about this?"

"No. It was a secret between your dad and us guys. I couldn't risk the news slipping out until I was ready to show ye the full vision." We start walking back downstairs to the first floor. He stops me to put the blindfold back on.

"Okay, here is the restaurant where we'll serve breakfast to our guests every morning," he says as he stops me to take the blindfold off. French doors are stenciled with the logo, *Dani's Café*. I have no words. Tears stream down my cheeks. Finn embraces me.

"You better buckle up because we're just getting started." He kisses my forehead. We finish walking the grounds and head toward the barn. As soon as we approach the side, he again blindfolds me.

"Are you ready?" he asks.

"I'm not sure. I'm already so blown away. How could you *possibly* have more?" I ask. He takes the blindfold off and attached to the side of the barn is a giant sign that reads *Hank's BBQ Heaven*.

"Are you *kidding* me?" I sob and he whispers how much he loves me in my ear. We stand there for several minutes before I can compose myself enough to enter for the tour. He explains the arrangement with Tex and how they had the dedication ceremony for Christie. Now the B&B makes much more sense since it sounds like we'll be relocating here to Austin full-time. He's thought of *everything*. He has completely recreated the ambience from our wedding. I comb over every detail. We swing through the kitchen and end in the office where he has yet another surprise. He has black and white poster-sized photos of Dan and Christine hanging on the wall. I gasp as soon as I see them.

"I thought they would bring us good luck," he says when Dani shouts, "Baba" and points at the posters on the wall. Finn and I are in utter shock and disbelief. Chills cover my entire body.

"Finn. . ." I step closer to the poster and prompt her again. "Dani, who is this?" I say, pointing at the poster of Dan.

"Baba," she says again without hesitation. She has a giant grin on her face and begins to gesture in sign language for more. We stand there at a complete loss for words. Reality sinks in. Dani really can see them. Danny and Christine are the imaginary friends. We questioned and wondered but neither of us allowed ourselves to go there. We didn't want to seem crazy.

Who would believe us? They've been with her since day one.

"Remember the toys moving that we couldn't explain? The smiling, giggling, and babbling? Wondering how she learned sign language and our confusion when we didn't know why she was asking for more? Her obsession with my charm bracelet? But her saying *Baba*? I mean . . . beyond comprehension," I say.

"In the best, most amazing way possible," Finn adds while we cover her in kisses. "We always knew you were special."

"She's been trying to tell us all along, haven't you, sweet baby?" I say. "I never told you this but when we couldn't explain things, I asked Danny for a sign. I told him he had to prove to me so I knew I wasn't crazy. I said it had to be bullet proof so there would be absolutely no doubt. The sign would have to be crystal clear and here it is. Wow," I say.

"This is our secret forever. The three musketeers."

"Good thing the media is on the way so they can get a close-up shot of me looking like a truck hit me. Good lord. Could I cry anymore?" I try to salvage whatever makeup I have left.

"*Wellllll*, there is one more thing," Finn says.

"Are you trying to kill me with happiness? 'Cause it's working," I joke.

"Why yes I am, my love." We pile back into the limo, he blindfolds me again, and we drive farther down into the property.

"Before we get out, I have something small for you to open." Finn hands me a small gift-wrapped box.

"I know you're not proposing so I can't imagine what this is." I open the box. There are three charms for my bracelet. A movie camera, a pig, and a key.

"A pig? You better start talking, mister, before this evening goes south in a hurry."

"I was looking for a charm to represent the new restaurant. Since it's BBQ, I got the pig and I think he looks like a Hank," he says.

"Okay . . . forgiven. But what's this key for?"

He gets out of the parked limo, walks around to open my door, and tells me to take the blindfold off but to keep my eyes closed. He hands me Dani, escorts us out, and positions us.

"It's for this. Now, open your eyes." My knees buckle; I'm so overwhelmed. I'm in complete and utter shock. *I can't believe he pulled this off.* All this time I thought he was just building a second restaurant. I was so wrapped up in my own world; I didn't ask many questions. I didn't think it was odd that he wasn't having me visit the site to witness progress. He kept telling me he wanted me to see the finished product so I respected his wishes. Never in my wildest dreams did I fathom he was creating a whole new world for us.

"Well, what do ye think?" he asks.

"It's not what I think but what I know. We're the luckiest girls in the world. Dani, look honey . . . *we're home.*"

www.ddmarx.com

CPSIA information can be obtained
at www.ICGtesting.com
Printed in the USA
LVOW03s0317011217
558260LV00009B/10/P